THE
AMERICAN HORSEWOMAN

BY
MRS. ELIZABETH KARR

PREFACE.

In presenting this volume to the women of America, the author would remark that, at least as far as she is aware, it is the first one, exclusively devoted to the instruction of lady riders, that has ever been written by one of their own countrywomen. In its preparation, no pretension is made to the style of a practiced author, the writer freely acknowledging it to be her first venture in the (to her) hitherto unexplored regions of authorship; she has simply undertaken,—being guided and aided by her own experience in horseback riding,—to write, in plain and comprehensive language, and in as concise a manner as is compatible with a clear understanding of her subject, all that she deems it essential for a horsewoman to know. This she has endeavored to do without any affectation or effort to acquire reputation as an author, and wholly for the purpose of benefiting those of her own sex who wish to learn not only to ride, but to ride well. She has also[iv] been induced to prepare the work by the urgent solicitations of many lady friends, who, desirous of having thorough information on horseback riding, were unable to find in any single work those instructions which they needed.

Many valuable works relating to the subject could be had, but none especially for ladies. True, in many of these works prepared for equestrians a few pages of remarks or advice to horsewomen could be found, but so scant and limited were they that but little useful and practical information could be gleaned from them. The writers of these works never even dreamed of treating many very important points highly essential to the horsewoman; and, indeed, it could hardly be expected that they would, as it is almost impossible for any horseman to know, much less to comprehend, these points. The position of a man in the saddle is natural and easy, while that of a woman is artificial, one-sided, and less readily acquired; that which he can accomplish with facility is for her impossible or extremely difficult, as her position lessens her command over the horse, and obliges her to depend almost entirely upon her skill and address for the means of controlling him.

If a gentleman will place himself upon the[v] side-saddle and for a short time ride the several gaits of his horse, he will have many points presented which he had not anticipated, and which may puzzle him; that which appeared simple and easy when in his natural position will become difficult of performance when he assumes the rôle of a horsewoman. A trial of this kind will demonstrate to him that the rules applicable to the one will not invariably be adapted to the other. The reader need not be surprised, therefore, if in the perusal of this volume she discovers in certain instances instructions laid down which differ from those met with in the popular works upon this subject by male authors.

Another inducement to prepare this volume existed in the fact that the ladies throughout the country, and especially in our large cities and towns, are apparently awakening to an appreciation of the importance of out-door amusement and exercise in securing and prolonging health, strength, beauty, and symmetry of form, and that horseback riding is rapidly becoming the favorite form of such exercise. Instructions relating to riding have become, therefore, imperative, in order to supply a need long felt by those horsewomen who, when in the saddle, are desirous of acquitting themselves[vi] with credit, but who have heretofore been unable to gain that information which would enable them to ride with ease and grace, and to manage their steeds with dexterity and confidence. The author—who has had several years' experience in horseback riding with the old-fashioned, two-pommeled saddle, and, in later years, with the English saddle, besides having had the benefit of the best continental teaching—believes she will be accused of neither vanity nor egotism when she states that within the pages of this work instructions will be found amply sufficient to enable any lady who attends to them to ride with artistic correctness.

Great care has been taken to enter upon and elucidate all those minute but important details which are so essential, but which, because they are so simple, are usually passed over without notice or explanation. Especial attention has also been given to the errors of inexperienced and uneducated riders, as well as to the mistakes into which beginners are apt to fall from incorrect modes of teaching, or from no instruction at all; these errors have been carefully pointed out, and the methods for correcting them explained. A constant effort has been made to have these practical hints and valuable[vii] explanations as lucid as possible, that they may readily be comprehended and put into practical use by the reader.

From the fact that considerable gossip, including some truth, as to illiteracy, rudeness, offensive familiarity, and scandal of various kinds has in past years been associated with some of the riding-schools established in our cities, many ladies entertain a decided antipathy to all riding-schools; to these ladies, as well as to those who are living in places where no riding-schools exist, the author feels confident that this work will prove of great practical utility. Yet she must remark that, in her opinion, it is neither just nor right to ostracize indiscriminately all such schools, simply because some of them have proven blameworthy; whenever a riding-school of good standing is established and is conducted by a well-known, competent, and gentlemanly teacher, with one or more skilled lady assistants, she would advise the ladies of the neighborhood to avail themselves of such opportunity to become sooner thorough and efficient horsewomen by pursuing the instructions given in this work under such qualified teachers.

ELIZABETH KARR.

NORTH BEND, OHIO.

[ix]

INTRODUCTION.

"How melts my beating heart as I behold
Each lovely nymph, our island's boast and pride,
Push on the generous steed, that sweeps along
O'er rough, o'er smooth, nor heeds the steepy hill,
Nor falters in the extended vale below!"

The Chase.

Among ladies of wealth and culture in England, the equestrienne art forms a portion of their education as much as the knowledge of their own language, of French, or of music, and great care is taken that their acquirements in this art shall be as thorough as those in any other branch of their tuition. The mother bestows much of her own personal supervision on her daughter's instruction, closely watching for every little fault, and promptly correcting it when any becomes manifest. As a result universally acknowledged, a young English lady, when riding a well-trained and spirited horse, is a sight at once elegant and attractive. She exhibits a degree of confidence, a firmness of seat, and an ease and grace that can be acquired only by the most careful and correct[2] instruction. The fair rider guides her steed, without abruptness, from walk to canter, from canter to trot, every movement in perfect harmony; horse and rider being, as it were, of one thought.

"Each look, each motion, awakes a new-born grace."

Unfortunately, at the present day, from want of careful study of the subject, the majority of American lady riders, notwithstanding the elegance of their forms and their natural grace, by no means equal their English sisters in the art of riding. In most instances, a faulty position in the saddle, an unsteadiness of seat, and a lack of sympathy between horse and rider, occasion in the mind of the spectator a sense of uneasiness lest the horse, in making playful movements, or, perhaps, becoming slightly fractious, may unseat his rider,—a feeling which quite destroys the charm and fascination she might otherwise exercise. If my countrywomen would but make a master stroke, and add correct horseback riding to the long list of accomplishments which they now possess, they would become irresistible, and while delighting others, would likewise promote their own physical well-being. There is no cosmetic nor physician's skill which can preserve the bloom and freshness of youth as riding can,[3]and my fair readers, if they wish to prolong those charms for which they are world renowned, charms whose only fault is their too fleeting existence, must take exercise, and be more in the fresh air and sunshine.

How much better to keep old age at bay by these innocent means, than to resort to measures which give to the eye of the world a counterfeit youth that will not deceive for a moment. Even an elderly lady may without offense or harsh criticism recall some of the past joys of younger years by an occasional ride for health or recreation, and, while gracefully accepting her half century, or more, of life, she can still retain some of the freshness and spirit of bygone years.

Not only is health preserved and life prolonged by exercise on horseback, but, in addition, sickness is banished, or meliorated, and melancholy, that dark demon which occasionally haunts even the most joyous life, is overcome and driven back to the dark shades from whence it came. Should the reader have the good fortune to possess an intelligent horse, she can, when assailed by sorrows real or fancied, turn to this true, willing friend, whose affectionate neigh of greeting as she approaches, and whose pretty little graceful arts, will tend[4] to dispel her gloom, and, once in the saddle, speeding along through the freshening air, fancied griefs are soon forgotten, while strength and nerve are gained to face those troubles of a more serious nature, whose existence cannot be ignored.

To the mistress who thoroughly understands the art of managing him, the horse gives his entire affection and obedience, becomes her most willing slave, submits to all her whims, and is proud and happy under her rule.

In disposition the horse is much like a child. Both are governed by kindness combined with firmness; both meet indifference with indifference, but return tenfold in love and obedience any care or affection that is bestowed upon them. The horse also resembles the child in the keenness with which he detects hypocrisy; no pretense of love or interest will impose on either.

To the lady rider who has neither real fondness for her horse nor knowledge of governing him, there is left but one resource by means of which the animal can be controlled, and this is the passion of fear. With a determined will, she may, by whipping, force him to obey, but this means is not always reliable, especially with a high-spirited animal, nor is it a method[5] which any true woman would care to employ. If, in addition to indifference to the horse, there be added nervousness and timidity, which she finds herself unable to overcome by practice and association, the lady might as well relinquish all attempt to become a rider.

Should any of my readers think that these views of the relations between horse and rider are too sentimental, that all which is needed in a horse is easy movement, obedience to the reins, and readiness to go forward when urged, and that love and respect are quite unnecessary, she will find, should she ever meet with any really alarming object on the road, that a little of this despised affection and confidence is very desirable, for, in the moment of danger, the voice which has never spoken in caressing accents, nor sought to win confidence will be unheeded; fear will prevail over careful training, and the rider will be very fortunate if she escapes without an accident. The writer is sustained in the idea that the affection of the horse is essential to the safety of the rider, not only by her own experience, but also by that of some of the most eminent teachers of riding, and trainers of horses.

Maud S. is an example of what a firm yet kind rule will effect in bringing forth the[6] capabilities of a horse. She has never had a harsh word spoken to her, and has never been punished with the whip, but has, on the contrary, been trained with the most patient and loving care; and the result has been a speed so marvelous as to have positively astonished the world, for although naturally high tempered, she will strain every nerve to please her kind, loving master, when urged forward by his voice alone.

Some ladies acquire a dislike for horseback riding, either because they experience discomfort or uneasiness when in the saddle, or because the movements of their horses cause them considerable fatigue. There may be various reasons for this: the saddle may be too large, or too small, or improperly made; or the rider's position in the saddle may be incorrect, and as a consequence, the animal cannot be brought to his best paces. Discomfort may occasionally be caused by an improperly made riding-habit. The rider whose waist is confined by tight lacing cannot adapt herself to the motions of her horse, and the graceful pliancy so essential to good riding will, therefore, be lost. The lady who wears tight corsets can never become a thorough rider, nor will the exercise of riding give her either pleasure or health. She may[7] manage to look well when riding at a gait no faster than a walk, but, beyond this, her motions will appear rigid and uncomfortable. A quick pace will induce rapid circulation, and the blood, checked at the waist, will, like a stream which has met with an obstacle in its course, turn into other channels, rushing either to the heart, causing faintness, or to the head, producing headache and vertigo. There have even been instances of a serious nature, where expectoration of blood has been occasioned by horseback riding, when the rider was tightly laced.

The naturally slender, symmetrical figure, when in the saddle, is the perfection of beauty, but she whom nature has endowed with more ample proportions will never attain this perfection by pinching her waist in. Let the full figure be left to nature, its owner sitting well in the saddle, on a horse adapted to her style, and she will make a very imposing appearance, and prove a formidable rival to her more slender companion.

There is a mistaken idea prevalent among certain persons, that horseback riding induces obesity. It is true that, to a certain extent, riding favors healthy muscular development, but the same may be said of all kinds of exercise,[8] and this effect, far from being objectionable, is highly desirable, as it contributes to symmetry of form, as well as to health and strength, conditions that in a large proportion of our American women are unfortunately lacking. Those who ride on horseback will find that while gaining in strength and proper physical tissue, they will, at the same time, as a rule, be gradually losing all excess of flesh; it is impossible for an active rider to become fat or flabby; but the indolent woman who is prejudiced against exercise of any kind will soon find the much dreaded calamity, corpulency, overtaking her, and beauty of form more or less rapidly disappearing beneath a mountain of flesh.

There are many persons who entertain the mistaken idea that instinct is a sufficient guide in learning to ride; that it is quite unnecessary to take any lessons or to make a study of the art of correct riding; and that youth, a good figure, and practice are all that is required to make a finished rider. This is a most erroneous opinion, which has been productive of much harm to lady riders. The above qualifications are undoubtedly great assistants, but without correct instruction they will never produce an accomplished and graceful rider.

The instinctive horsewoman usually rides[9] boldly and with perfect satisfaction to herself, but to the eye of the connoisseur she presents many glaring defects. Very bold, but, at the same time, very bad riding is often seen among those who consider themselves very fine horsewomen. In order to gain the reputation of a finished rider, it is not essential that one should perform all the antics of a circus rider, nor that she should ride a Mazeppian horse. The finished rider may be known by the correctness of her attitude in the saddle, by her complete control of her horse, and by the tranquillity of her motions when in city or park; in such places she makes no attempt to ride at a very rapid trot, or flying gallop-gaits which should be reserved for country roads, where more speed is allowable.

There is still another false idea prevalent among a certain class of people, which is that a love for horses, and for horseback riding necessarily makes one coarse, and detracts from the refinement of a woman's nature. It must be acknowledged that the coarseness of a vulgar spirit can be nowhere more conspicuously displayed than in the saddle, and yet in no place is the delicacy and decorum of woman more observable. A person on horseback is placed in a position where every motion is subject[10] to critical observation and comment. The quiet, simple costume, the easy movements, the absence of ostentatious display, will always proclaim the refined, well-bred rider. Rudeness in the saddle is as much out of place as in the parlor or salon, and greatly more annoying to spectators, besides being disrespectful and dangerous to other riders. Abrupt movements, awkward and rapid paces, frequently cause neighboring horses to become restless, and even to run away. Because a lady loves her horse, and enjoys riding him, it is by no means necessary that she should become a Lady Gay Spanker, indulge in stable talk, make familiars of grooms and stable boys, or follow the hounds in the hunting field.

There are in this work no especial instructions given for the hunting field, as the author does not consider it a suitable place for a lady rider. She believes that no lady should risk life and limb in leaping high and dangerous obstacles, but that all such daring feats should be left to the other sex or to circus actresses. Nor would any woman who really cared for her horse wish to run the risk of reducing him to the deplorable condition of many horses that follow the hounds. In England, where hunting is the favorite pastime among gentlemen, the[11] number of maimed and crippled horses that one meets is disheartening. Every lady, however, who desires to become a finished rider, should learn to leap, as this will not only aid her in securing a good seat in the saddle, but may also prove of value in times of danger.

Before concluding I would again urge upon my readers the importance of out-of-door exercise, which can hardly be taken in a more agreeable form than that of horseback riding,—a great panacea, giving rest and refreshment to the overworked brain of the student, counteracting many of the pernicious effects of the luxurious lives of the wealthy, and acting upon the workers of the world as a tonic, and as a stimulus to greater exertion.

[13]

THE AMERICAN HORSEWOMAN.

CHAPTER I.
THE HORSE.

"Look, when a painter would surpass the life,
In limning out a well-proportioned steed,
His art with Nature's workmanship at strife,
As if the dead the living should exceed;
So did this horse excel a common one,
In shape, in courage, color, pace, and bone."
. . . .
—"what a horse should have he did not lack,
Save a proud rider on so proud a back."

Venus and Adonis.

It is supposed that the original home of the horse was central Asia, and that all the wild horses that range over the steppes of Tartary, the pampas of South America, and the prairies of North America, are descendants of this Asiatic stock.[1] There is, in the history of the [14] world, no accurate statement of the time when the horse was first subjugated by man, but so far back as his career can be traced in the dim and shadowy past, he seems to have been man's servant and companion. We find him, on the mysterious ruins of ancient Egypt, represented with his badge of servitude, the bridle; he figures in myth and fable as the companion of man and gods; he is a prominent figure in the pictured battle scenes of the ancient world; and has always been a favorite theme with poet, historian, and philosopher in all ages.

The first written record, known to us, of the subjection of the horse to man is found in the Bible, where in Genesis (xlvii. 17) it is stated that Joseph gave the Egyptians bread in exchange for their horses, and in 1. 9, we read that when Joseph went to bury his father Jacob, there went with him the servants of the house of Pharaoh, the elders of the land of Egypt, together with "chariots and horsemen" in numbers. Jeremiah compares the speed of the horse with the swiftness of the eagle; and Job's description of the war charger has never been surpassed.

Ancient Rome paid homage to the horse by a [15] yearly festival, when every one abstained from labor, and the day was made one of feasting and frolic. The horse, decked with garlands, and with gay and costly trappings, was led in triumph through the streets, followed by a multitude who loudly proclaimed in verse and song his many good services to man.

This adulation of the horse sometimes went beyond the bounds of reason, as in the case of Caligula, who carried his love for his horse, Incitatus, to an insane degree. He had a marble palace erected for a stable, furnished it with mangers of ivory and gold, and had sentinels guard it at night that the repose of his favorite might not be disturbed. Another elegant palace was fitted up in the most splendid and costly style, and here the animal's visitors were entertained. Caligula required all who called upon himself to visit Incitatus also, and to treat the animal with the same respect and reverence as that observed towards a royal host. This horse was frequently introduced at Caligula's banquets, where he was presented with gilded oats, and with wine from a golden cup. Historians state that Caligula would even have made his steed consul of Rome, had not the tyrant been opportunely assassinated, and the world freed from an insane fiend.

[16]

In the legends of the Middle Ages the knight-errant and his gallant steed were inseparable, and together performed doughty deeds of valor and chivalry. In our present more prosaic age, the horse has been trained to such a degree of perfection in speed and motion as was never dreamed of by the ancients or by the knights of the crusades; and there has been given to the world an animal that is a marvel of courage, swiftness, and endurance, while, at the same time, so docile, that the delicate hand of woman can completely control him.

The Arabian is the patrician among horses; he is the most intelligent, the most beautifully formed, and, when kindly treated, the gentlest of his race. He is especially noted for his keenness of perception, his retentive memory, his powers of endurance, and, when harshly or cruelly treated, for his fierce resentment and ferociousness, which nothing but death can conquer. In his Arabian home he is guarded as a treasure, is made one of the family and treated with the most loving care. This close companionship creates an affection and confidence between the horse and his master which is almost unbounded; while the kindness with which the animal is treated seems to brighten his intelligence as well as to render him gentle.

[17]

When these horses were first introduced into Europe they seemed, after a short stay in civilization, to have completely changed their nature, and, instead of gentleness and docility, exhibited an almost tiger-like ferocity. This change was at first attributed to difference of climate and high feeding, but, after several grooms had been injured or killed by their charges, it began to be suspected that there was something wrong in the treatment. The experiment of introducing native grooms was therefore tried, and the results proved most satisfactory, the animals once more becoming gentle and docile.[2] Since then the nature of the Arabian has become better understood, and,[18] both in this country and in Europe, he shows, at the present day, a decided improvement upon the original native of the desert. He is larger and swifter, yet still retains all the spirit as well as docility of his ancestors. In America his descendants are called "thorough-breds," and Americans may well be proud of this race of horses, which is rapidly becoming world renowned.

Before purchasing a saddle-horse, several points should be considered. First, **the style of the rider's figure**; for a horse which would be suitable for a large, stout person would not be at all desirable for one having a small, slender figure. A large, majestic looking woman would present a very absurd spectacle when mounted upon a slightly built, slender horse; his narrow back in contrast with that of his rider would cause hers to appear even larger and wider than usual, and thus give her a heavy and ridiculous appearance, while the little horse would look overburdened and miserable, and his step, being too short for his rider, would cause her to experience an unpleasant sensation of embarrassment and restraint. On the other hand, a short, light, slender rider, seated upon a[19] tall broad-backed animal, would appear equally out of place; the step of the horse being, in her case, too long, would make her seat unsteady and insecure, so that instead of a sense of enjoyment, exhilaration, and benefit from the ride, she would experience only fatigue and dissatisfaction.

If the rider be tall and rather plump, the horse should be fifteen hands and three inches in height, and have a somewhat broad back. A lady below the medium height, and of slender proportions, will look equally well when riding a pony fourteen hands high, or a horse fifteen hands. An animal fifteen hands, or fifteen hands and two inches in height, will generally be found suitable for all ladies who are not excessively large and tall, or very short and slender. In all cases, however, the back of the horse should be long enough to appear well under the side-saddle, for a horse with a short back never presents a fine aspect when carrying a woman. In such cases, the side-saddle extends from his withers nearly, if not quite, to his hips, and as the riding skirt covers his left side, little is seen of the horse except his head and tail. Horses with very short backs are usually good weight-carriers, but their gaits are apt to be rough and uneasy.

[20]

Another point to be considered in the selection of a horse is, what gait or gaits are best suited to the rider, and here again the lady should take her figure into consideration. The walk, trot, canter, and gallop are the only gaits recognized by English horsewomen, but in America the walk, rack, pace, and canter are the favorite gaits. If the lady's figure be slender and elegant, any of the above named gaits will suit her, but should she be large or stout, a brisk walk or easy canter should be selected. The rapid gallop and all fast gaits should be left to light and active riders.

The fast or running walk is a very desirable gait for any one, but is especially so for middle-aged or stout people, who cannot endure much jolting; it is also excellent for delicate women, for poor riders, or for those who have long journeys to make which they wish to accomplish speedily and without undue fatigue to themselves or their horses. A good sound horse who has been trained to this walk can readily travel thirty or forty miles a day, or even more. This gait is adapted equally well to the street, the park, and the country road; but it must be acknowledged that horses possessing it rarely have any other that is desirable, and, indeed, any other would be apt to impair the ease and[21] harmony of the animal's movements in this walk.

The French or cavalry trot (see page 203) should never be ridden on the road by a woman, as the movements of the horse in this gait are so very rough that the most accomplished rider cannot keep a firm, steady seat. The body is jolted in a peculiar and very unpleasant manner, occasioning a sense of fatigue that is readily appreciated, though difficult to describe.

The country jog-trot is another very fatiguing gait, although farmers, who ride it a good deal, state that "after one gets used to it, it is not at all tiresome." But a lady's seat in the saddle is so different from that of a gentleman's that she can never ride this gait without excessive fatigue.

A rough racker or pacer will prove almost as wearisome as the jog-trotter. Indeed, if she wishes to gain any pleasure or benefit from riding, a lady should never mount a horse that is at all stiff or uneven in his movements, no matter what may be his gait.

The easiest of all gaits to ride, although the most difficult to learn, is the English trot. This is especially adapted to short persons, who can ride it to perfection. A tall woman will be apt to lean too far forward when rising in it, and[22] her specialties, therefore, should be the canter and the gallop, in which she can appear to the greatest advantage. The rack, and the pace of a horse that has easy movements are not at all difficult to learn to ride, and are, consequently, the favorite gaits of poor riders.

In selecting a horse his **temperament** must also be considered. A high-spirited, nervous animal, full of vitality, highly satisfactory as he might prove to some, would be only a source of misery to others of less courageous dispositions. First lessons in riding should be taken upon a horse of cold temperament and kindly disposition who will resent neither mistakes nor awkwardness. Having learned to ride and to manage a horse properly, no steed can then be too mettlesome for the healthy and active lady pupil, provided he has no vices and possesses the good manners that should always belong to every lady's horse.

It is a great mistake to believe, as many do, that a weak, slightly built horse is yet capable of carrying a woman. On the contrary, a lady's horse should be the soundest and best that can be procured, and should be able to carry with perfect ease a weight much greater than hers. A slight, weak animal, if ridden much by a woman, will be certain to "get out of condition,"[23] will become unsound in the limbs of one side, usually the left, and will soon wear out.

Before buying a horse, the lady who is to ride him should be weighed, and should then have some one who is considerably heavier than herself ride the animal, that she may be sure that her own weight will not be too great for him. If he carries the heavier weight with ease, he can, of course, carry her.

In selecting a horse great care should be taken to ascertain whether there is the least trace of **unsoundness in his feet and legs**, and especially that variety of unsoundness which occasions stumbling. The best of horses, when going over rough places or when very tired may stumble, and so will indolent horses that are too lazy when traveling to lift their feet up fully; but when this fault is due to disease, or becomes a habit with a lazy animal, he should never be used under the side-saddle.

Fig. 1.—Head of Arabian Steed.

Fig. 2.—Head of Low-Bred Horse.

If the reader will glance at Figs. 1 and 2, she will observe the difference between the head of the low-bred horse and that of the best bred of the race. Fig. 1 represents the head of an Arabian horse; the brain is wide between the eyes, the brow high and prominent, and the expression of the face high-bred and intelligent. Fig. 2 shows the head of a low-bred horse, whose[24] stupid aspect and small brain are very manifest. The one horse will be quick to comprehend what is required of him, and will appreciate any efforts made to brighten his intelligence, while the other will be slow to understand, almost indifferent to the kindness of his master, and apt, when too much indulged, to return treachery for good treatment. The whip, when applied to the latter as a means of punishment, will probably cow him, but, if used for the same purpose on the former, will rouse in him all the hot temper derived from his ancestors, and in the contest which ensues between his master and himself, he will conquer, or terminate the strife his own death, or that of his master.

[25]

Another noticeable feature in the Arab horse, and one usually considered significant of an active and wide-awake temperament, is the width and expansiveness of the nostrils. These, upon the least excitement, will quiver and expand, and in a rapid gallop will stand out freely, giving a singularly spirited look to the animal's face.

The shape and size of the ears are also indications of high or low birth. In the high-bred horse they are generally small, thin, and delicate on their outer margins, with the tips inclined somewhat towards one another. By means of these organs the animal expresses his different emotions of anger, fear, dislike, or gayety. They may be termed his language, and their various movements can readily be understood when one takes a little trouble to study their indications. The ears of a low-bred horse are large, thick, and covered with coarse hair; they sometimes lop or droop horizontally, protruding from the sides of the head and giving a very sheepish look to the face; they rarely move, and express very little emotion of any kind.

The eye of the desert steed is very beautiful, possessing all the brilliancy and gentleness so much admired in that of the gazelle. Its expression[26] in repose is one of mildness and amiability, but, under the influence of excitement, it dilates widely and sparkles. A horse which has small eyes set close together, no matter what excellences he may possess in other respects, is sure to have some taint of inferior blood. Some of the coarser breeds have the large eye of the Arabian, but it will usually be found that they have some thorough-bred among their ancestors.

Fig. 3.—Width of lower jaw in the thorough-bred.

Width between the sides or branches of the lower jaw is another distinctive feature of the horse of pure descent. (Fig. 3.) A wide furrow or channel between the points mentioned is necessary for speed, in order to allow room for free respiration when the animal is in rapid motion. The coarser breeds have very small, narrow channels (Fig. 4), and very rapid motion soon distresses them.

Fig. 4.—Width of lower jaw in the low-bred.

The mouth of the well-bred horse is large, allowing ample room for the bit, and giving him a determined and energetic, but at the same time pleasant,[27] amiable expression. The mouth of the low-bred horse is small and covered with coarse hair, and gives the animal a sulky, dejected appearance.

Fig. 5.—Oblique shoulder.
The angle at the joint being about 45°.

The light, elegant head of the Arabian is well set on his neck; a slight convexity at the upper part of the throat gives freedom to the functions of this organ, as well as elasticity to the movements of the head and neck; and the *encolure*, or crest of the neck, is arched with a graceful curve. But it is especially in the shape of the shoulders that this horse excels all others, and this is the secret of those easy movements which make him so desirable for the saddle. These shoulders are deep, and placed obliquely at an angle of about 45°; they act like the springs of a well-made carriage, diminishing the shock or jar of his movements. They are always accompanied by a deep chest, high withers, and fore-legs set well forward, qualities which make the horse much safer for riding. (Fig. 5.)

Fig. 6.—Straight or upright shoulder.
The angle at the joint being more than 45°.

The animal with straight shoulders, no matter how well shaped in other respects, can never make a good saddle-horse, and should be at[28] once rejected. These shoulders are usually accompanied by low withers, and fore-legs placed too far under the body, which arrangement causes the rider an unpleasant jar every time a fore-foot touches the ground. Moreover, the gait of the horse is constrained and not always safe, and if he be used much under the saddle his fore-feet will soon become unsound. This straight, upright shoulder is characteristic of the coarser breeds of horses, and is frequently associated with a short, thick neck. Such horses are not only unfit for the saddle, but, when any speed is desired, are unsuitable even for a pleasure carriage. (Fig. 6.)

The haunch of the low-bred horse is generally large, but not so well formed as that of the thorough-bred. This portion of the Arabian courser is wide, indicating strength, and force to propel himself forward, while his tail, standing out gayly when he is in motion, projects in a line with his back-bone. His forearm is large, long, and muscular,[3] his knees broad and firm,[29] his hocks of considerable size, while his cannon-bone, situated between the knee and the fetlock, is short, although presenting a broad appearance when viewed laterally.

On each front leg, at the back of the knee, there is a bony projection, giving attachments to the flexor muscles, and affording protection to certain tendons. The Orientals set a great value upon the presence of this bone, believing that it favors muscular action, and the larger this prominence is the more highly do they prize the animal that possesses it. The pasterns of the high-bred horse are of medium length, and very elastic, while the foot is circular and of moderate size.

In the preceding description, the author has endeavored to make plain to the reader the most important points to be observed in both the high-bred and the low-bred horse, and has given the most pronounced characteristics of each.

[30]

Between these extremes, however, there are many varieties of horses, possessing more or less of the Arabian characteristics mingled with those of other races. Some of the best American horses are numbered among these mixed races, and, by many, are considered an improvement upon the Arabian, as they are excellent for light carriages and buggies. The more they resemble the Oriental steed, the better they are for the saddle.

The lady who, in this country, cannot find a horse to suit her, will, indeed, be difficult to please. It will be best for her to tell some gentleman what sort of horse she wishes, and let him select for her; but, at the same time, it can do no harm, and may prove a great advantage to her to know all the requisite points of a good saddle-horse. It will not take long to learn them, and the knowledge gained will prevent her from being imposed upon by the ignorant or unscrupulous. Gentlemen, even those who consider themselves good judges of horse-flesh, are sometimes guilty of very serious blunders in selecting a horse for a lady's use; and should the lady be obliged to negotiate directly with a horse-dealer, she must bear in mind constantly the fact that, although there are reliable and honorable dealers to be found,[31] there are many who would not scruple to cheat even a woman. A careful perusal of the present work, together with the advice of an *upright* and *trustworthy* veterinary surgeon, or a skilled riding-master, will aid her in protecting herself from the impositions of unprincipled horse-jockeys and self-styled "veterinary doctors."

In any case, whatever be the other characteristics of the animal selected, be sure that he has the oblique shoulder, as well as depth of shoulder, and hind-legs well bent. Without these characteristics he will be unfit for a lady's use, as his movements will be rough and unsafe, and the saddle will be apt to turn.

If it be desired to purchase a horse for a moderate price, certain points which might be insisted on in a high-priced animal will have to be dispensed with; for instance, his color may not be satisfactory; he may not have a pretty head, or a well-set tail, etc., but these deficiencies may be overlooked if he be sound, have good action, and no vices. He may be handsome, well-actioned, and thoroughly trained, but have a slight defect in his wind, noticeable only when he is urged into a rapid trot, or a gallop. If wanted for street and park service only, and if the purchaser does not care for fast[32] riding, a horse of this sort will suit her very well. Sometimes a horse of good breed, as well as of good form, has never had the advantages of a thorough training, or he may be worn out by excessive work. Should he be comparatively young, rest and proper training may still make a good horse of him, but great care should be taken to assure one's self that no permanent disease or injury exists. The Orientals have a proverb, that it is well to bear in mind when buying an animal of the kind just described:—"Ruin, son of ruin, is he who buys to cure."

Always examine with great care a horse's mouth. A hard-mouthed animal is a very unpleasant one for a lady to ride, and is apt to degenerate into a runaway. Scars at the angles of the mouth are good indications of a "bolter," or runaway, or at least of cruel treatment, and harsh usage is by no means a good instructor.

While a very short-backed horse does not appear to great advantage under a side-saddle, he may, nevertheless, have many good qualities that will compensate for this defect, and it may be overlooked provided the price asked for him be reasonable; but horses of this kind frequently command a high price when their action is exceptionally good. Corns on the feet generally depreciate the value of a horse, although[33] they may sometimes be cured by removing the shoes, and giving him a free run of six or eight months in a pasture of soft ground; if he be then properly shod, and used on country roads only, he may become permanently serviceable. There is, however, considerable risk in buying a horse that has corns, and the purchaser should remember the Oriental proverb just referred to, and not forget the veterinary surgeon.

Before paying for a horse, the lady should insist upon having him on trial for at least a month, that she may have an opportunity of discovering his vices or defects, if any such exist. She must be careful not to condemn him too hastily, and should, when trying him, make due allowance for his change of quarters and also for the novelty of carrying a new rider, as some horses are very nervous until they become well acquainted with their riders. Should the horse's movements prove rough, should he be found hard-mouthed, or should any indications of unsoundness or viciousness be detected, he should be immediately returned to his owner. It must be remembered, however, that very few horses are perfect, and that minor defects may, in most instances, be overlooked if the essentials are secured. Before rejecting the horse,[34] the lady should also be very sure that the faults to which she objects are not due to her own mismanagement of him. But if she decides that she is not at fault, no amount of persuasion should induce her to purchase. In justice to the owner of the horse, he ought to be reasonably paid for the time and services of his rejected animal; but if it be decided to keep the horse, then only the purchase-money originally agreed upon should be paid.

The surest and best way of securing a good saddle-horse is to purchase, from one of the celebrated breeding farms, a well-shaped four-year-old colt of good breed, and have him taught the gaits and style of movement required. Great care should be taken in the selection of his teacher, for if the colt's temper be spoiled by injudicious treatment, he will be completely ruined for a lady's use. A riding-school teacher will generally understand all the requirements necessary for a lady's saddle-horse, and may be safely intrusted with the animal's education. If no riding-school master of established reputation as a trainer can be had, it may be possible to secure the services of some one near the lady's home, as she can then superintend the colt's education herself and be sure that he is treated neither rashly nor cruelly.

[35]

The ideas concerning the education of the horse have completely changed within the last twenty-five years. The whip as a means of punishment is entirely dispensed with in the best training schools of the present day, and, instead of rough and brutal measures, kindness, firmness, and patience are now the only means employed to train and govern him. The theory of this modern system of training may be found in the following explanation of a celebrated English trainer, who subdued his horses by exhibiting towards them a wonderful degree of patience:—"If I enter into a contest with the horse, he will fling and prance, and there will be no knowing which will be master; whereas if I remain quiet and determined, I have the best of it."

The following is an example of the patience with which this man carried out his theory:—

Being once mounted on a very obstinate colt that refused to move in the direction desired, he declined all suggestions of severe measures, and after one or two gentle but fruitless attempts to make the animal move, he desisted, and having called for his pipe, sat there quietly for a couple of hours enjoying a good smoke, and chatting gayly with passing friends. Then after another quiet but unsuccessful attempt[36] to induce the colt to move, he sent for some dinner which he ate while still on the animal's back. As night approached and the air became cool, he sent for his overcoat and more tobacco, and proceeded to make a night of it. About this time the colt became uneasy, but not until midnight did he show any disposition to move in the required direction. Now was the time for the master to assert himself. "Whoa!" he cried, "you have stayed here so long to please yourself, now you will stay a little longer to please me." He then kept the colt standing in the same place an hour longer, and when he finally allowed him to move, it was in a direction opposite to that which the colt seemed disposed to take. He walked the animal slowly for five miles, then allowed him to trot back to his stable, and finally—as if he had been a disobedient child—sent him supperless to bed, giving him the rest of the night in which to meditate upon the effects of his obstinacy.

To some this may seem a great deal of useless trouble to take with a colt that might have been compelled to move more promptly by means of whip or spur; but that day's experience completely subdued the colt's stubborn spirit, and all idea of rebellion to human authority was banished from his mind forever.[37] Had a contrary course been pursued, it would probably have made the creature headstrong, balky, and unreliable; he would have yielded to the whip and spur at one time only to battle the more fiercely against them at the first favorable opportunity, and his master would never have known at what minute he might have to enter into a contest with him. That a horse trained by violent means can never be trusted is a fact which is every day becoming better recognized and appreciated.

"A great many accidents might be avoided," says a well-known authority upon the education of the horse, "could the populace be instructed to think a horse was endowed with senses, was gifted with feelings, and was able in some degree to appreciate motives."... "The strongest man cannot physically contend against the weakest horse. Man's power reposes in better attributes than any which reside in thews and muscles. Reason alone should dictate and control his conduct. Thus guided, mortals have subdued the elements. For power, when mental, is without limit: by savage violence nothing is attained and man is often humbled."

The lady who has the good fortune to live in the country where she can have so many opportunities for studying the disposition and [38] character of her animals, and can, if she chooses, watch and superintend the education of her horse from the time he is a colt, has undoubtedly a better chance of securing a fine saddle-horse than she who lives in the city and is obliged to depend almost entirely upon others for the training of her horse. Indeed, very little formal training will be necessary for a horse that has been brought up under the eye of a kind and judicious mistress, for he will soon learn to understand and obey the wishes of one whom he loves and trusts, and if she be an accomplished rider she can do the greater part of the training herself.

The best and most trustworthy horse the author ever had was one that was trained almost from his birth. Fay's advent was a welcome event to the children of the family, by whom he was immediately claimed and used as a play-fellow. By the older members of the family he was always regarded as part of the household,—an honored servant, to be well cared for,—and he was petted and fondled by all, from paterfamilias down to Bridget in the kitchen. He was taught, among other tricks, to bow politely when anything nice was given him, and many were the journeys he made around to the kitchen window, where he would make [39] his obeisance in such an irresistible manner that Bridget would be completely captivated; and the dainty bits were passed through the window in such quantities and were swallowed with such avidity that the lady of the house had to interfere and restrict the donations to two cakes daily.

Fay had been taught to shake hands with his admirers, and this trick was called his "word of honor;" he had his likes and dislikes, and would positively refuse to honor some people with a hand-shake. If these slighted individuals insisted upon riding him, he made them so uncomfortable by the roughness of his gaits that they never cared to repeat the experiment. But the favored ones, whom he had received into his good graces and to whom he had given his "word of honor," he would carry safely anywhere, at his lightest and easiest gait. Fay never went back on his word, which is more than can be said of some human beings.

The great difficulty in training a horse for a lady's use is to get him well placed on his haunches. In Fay's case this was accomplished by teaching him to place his fore-feet upon a stout inverted tub, about two feet high. When he offered his "hand" for a shake, some one pushed forward the tub, upon which his "foot" [40] dropped and was allowed to remain a short time, when the other foot was treated in the same manner. After half a dozen lessons of this sort, he learned to put up his feet without assistance; first one, and then the other, and, finally, both at once. These performances were always rewarded by a piece of apple or cake, together with expressions of pleasure from the by-standers. Fay had a weakness for flattery, and no actor called before the curtain ever expressed more pleasure at an *encore* than did Fay when applauded for his efforts to please. That the tub trick would prove equally effectual with other horses in teaching them to place themselves well on their haunches cannot be positively stated. It might prove more troublesome to teach most horses this trick than to have them placed upon their haunches in the usual way by means of a strong curb, or by lessons with the lunge line. It proved entirely successful in Fay's case, and a horse lighter in hand or easier in gait was never ridden by a woman.

Fay's training began when he was only a few weeks old: a light halter and a loose calico surcingle were placed on him for a short time each day, during which time he was carefully watched lest he should do himself some injury. When [41] he was about eight months old, a small bit, made of a smooth stick of licorice, was put into his mouth, and to this bit light leather reins were fastened by pieces of elastic rubber: this rubber relieved his mouth from a constant dead pull, and tended to preserve its delicate sensibility. Thus harnessed he was led around the lawn, followed by a crowd of youthful admirers and playmates, who formed a sort of triumphal procession, with which the colt was as well pleased as the spectators. Every attempt on his part to indulge in horse-play, such as biting, kicking, etc., was always quickly checked, and no one was allowed to tease or strike him.

Nothing heavier than a dumb jockey was put on his back until he was four years old, when his education began in sober earnest. After a few lessons with the lunge line, given by a regular trainer, a saddle was put on his back, and for the first time in his life he carried a human being.

When learning his different riding gaits on the road, he was always accompanied by a well-trained saddle-horse, aided by whose example as well as by the efforts of his rider he was soon trained in three different styles of movement, namely, a good walk, trot, and hand gallop. Fear seemed unknown to this horse, for he had[42] always been allowed as a colt to follow his dam on the road, and had thus become so accustomed to all such alarming objects as steam engines, hay carts, etc., that they had ceased to occasion him the least uneasiness. This high spirited and courageous animal had perfect confidence in the world and looked upon all mankind as friendly. His constant companionship with human beings had sharpened his perceptive faculties, and made him quick to understand whatever was required of him. The kindness shown him was never allowed to degenerate into weakness or over-indulgence, and whenever anything was required of him it was insisted upon until complete obedience was obtained. In this way he was taught to understand that man was his master and superior.

Although it is not absolutely essential that a lady's horse should learn the tricks of bowing, hand-shaking, etc., yet the lady who will take the pains to teach her horse some of them will find that she not only gets a great deal of pleasure from the lessons, but that they enable her to gain more complete control over him, for the horse, like some other animals, gives affection and entire obedience to the person who makes an effort to increase his intelligence.

Lessons with the lunge line should always be[43] short, as they are very fatiguing to a young colt, and when given too often or for too great a length of time they make him giddy from rush of blood to the head; not a few instances, indeed, have occurred where a persistence in such lessons has occasioned complete blindness.

A lady's horse should be taught to disregard the flapping of the riding-skirt, and it is also well for him to become accustomed to having articles of various kinds, such as pieces of cloth, paper, etc., fluttering about him, as he will not then be likely to take fright should any part of the rider's costume become disarranged and blow about him.

He should also be so trained that he will not mind having the saddle moved from side to side on his back. The best of riders may have her saddle turn, and if the horse be thus trained he will neither kick nor run away should such an accident occur.

It is also very important that the horse should be taught to stop, and stand as firm as a rock at the word of command given in a low, firm tone. This habit is not only important in mounting and dismounting,—feats which it is difficult, if not impossible, for the lady to perform unless the horse be perfectly still,—but the rider will also find this prompt obedience of[44] great assistance in checking her horse when he becomes frightened and tries to break away; for he will stop instinctively when he hears the familiar order given in the voice to which he is accustomed.

A lady should not fail to visit her horse's stable from time to time, in order to assure herself that he is well treated and properly cared for by the groom. Viciousness and restlessness on the road can often be traced to annoyances and ill-treatment in the stable. Grooms and stable boys sometimes like to see the horse kick out and attempt to bite, and will while away their idle hours in harassing him, tickling his ears with straws, or touching him up with the whip in order to make him prance and strike out. The result of these annoyances will be that, if the lady during her ride accidentally touches her horse with the whip, he will begin prancing and kicking; or, if it is summer time, the gnats and flies swarming about his ears will make him unmanageable. In the latter case, ear-tips will only make the matter worse, especially if they have dangling tassels. When such signs of nervousness are noticeable, especially in a horse that has been hitherto gentle, they may usually be attributed to the treatment of the groom or his assistants.

[45]

Most grooms delight in currying their charges with combs having teeth like small spikes and in laying on the polishing brush with a hand as heavy as the blows of misfortune. Some animals, it is true, like this kind of rubbing, but there are many, who have thin, delicate skins, to whom such treatment is almost unmitigated torture. Should the lady hear any contest going on between the horse and groom during the former's morning toilette, she should order a blunt curry-comb to be used; or even dispense with a comb altogether, and let the brush only be applied with a light hand. Grooms sometimes take pleasure in throwing cold water over their horses. In very warm weather, and when the animal is not overheated, this treatment may prove refreshing to him, but, as a general rule it is objectionable, as it is apt to occasion a sudden chill which may result in serious consequences.

The stable man may grumble at the lady's interference and supervision, but she must not allow this to prevent her from attending carefully to the welfare of the animal whose faithful services contribute so largely to her pleasure. When she buys a horse she introduces a new member into her household, who should be as well looked after and cared for as any other[46] faithful servant or friend. Indeed, the horse is the more entitled to consideration in that he is entirely helpless, and his lot for good or evil lies wholly in her power. If the mistress is careless or neglects her duty, the servants in whose charge the horse is placed will be very apt to follow her example, and the poor animal will suffer accordingly.

Perhaps the lady, however, may object to entering the stable, and agree with the groom in thinking it "no place for a woman." Or she may fear that in carrying out the ideas suggested above she will expose herself to the ridicule of thoughtless acquaintances who can never do anything until it has received the sanction of fashion.

For the benefit of this fastidious individual and her timid friends we will quote the example of the Empress of Austria, who, although occupying an exalted position at a court where etiquette is carried to the extremes of formality, yet does not hesitate to visit the stable of her favorite steeds and personally to supervise their welfare; and woe to the perverse groom who in the least particular disobeys her commands.

Many other examples might be given of high-born ladies, such as Queen Victoria, the Princess of Wales, the Princess of Prussia, and[47] others, who do not seem to consider it at all unfeminine or coarse for a woman to give some personal care and supervision to her horses. But to enter into more details would prove tiresome, and the example given is enough to silence the scruples of the followers of fashion.

Like all herbivorous creatures that love to roam in herds, the horse is naturally of a restless temperament. Activity is the delight of his existence, and when left to nature and a free life he is seldom quiet. Man takes this creature of buoyant nature from the freedom of its natural life, and confines the active body in a prison house where its movements are even more circumscribed than are those of the wild beasts in the menagerie; they can at least turn around and walk from side to side in their cages, but the horse in his narrow stall is able only to move his head from side to side, to paw a little with his fore-feet, and to move backwards and forwards a short distance, varying with the length of his halter; when he lies down to sleep he is compelled to keep in one position, and runs the risk of meeting with some serious accident. In some stables where the grooms delight in general stagnation, the horses under their charge are not allowed to indulge in even the smallest liberty. The slightest movement[48] is punished by the lash of these silence-loving tyrants, in whose opinion the horse has enough occupation and excitement in gazing at the blank boards directly in front of his head. If these boards should happen to be whitewashed, as is often the case in the country, constant gazing at them will be almost sure to give rise to shying, or even to occasion blindness. If the reader will, for several minutes, gaze steadily at a white wall, she will he able to get some idea of the poor horse's sensations.

Is it then to be wondered at, that an animal of an excitable nature like the horse should, when released from the oppressive quiescence of his prison-house, act as if bereft of reason, and perform strange antics and caperings in his insane delight at once more breathing the fresh air, and seeing the outside world. But, while the horse is thus expressing his pleasure and recovering the use of limbs by vigorous kicks, or is expending his superfluous energy by bounding out of the road at every strange object he encounters, the saddle will be neither a safe nor pleasant place for the lady rider. To avoid such danger, and to compensate, in some degree, the liberty-loving animal for depriving him of his natural life and placing him in bondage, he should be given, instead of[49] the usual narrow stall, a box stall, measuring about sixteen or eighteen feet square. In this box the horse should be left entirely free, without even a halter, as this appendage has sometimes been the cause of fearful accidents, by becoming entangled with the horse's feet.

The groom may grumble again at this innovation, because a box stall means more work for him, but if he really cares for the horses under his charge he will soon become reconciled to the small amount of extra work required by the use of a box stall. Every one who knows anything about a horse in the stable is well aware of the injury done to this animal's feet and limbs by compelling him to stand always confined to one spot in a narrow stall. A box will prevent the occurrence of these injuries, besides giving the horse a little freedom and enabling him to get more rest and benefit from his sleep.

Some horses are fond of looking through a window or over a half door. The glimpse they thus get of the outside life seems to amuse and interest them, and it can do no harm to gratify this desire. Others, however, seem to be worried and excited by such outlooks; they become restless and even make attempts to leap over the half door or through the window. In such[50] cases there should, of course, be no out-of-door scenery visible from the box.

The groom should exercise the horse daily, in a gentle and regular manner; an hour or two of walking, varied occasionally by a short trot, will generally be found sufficient. Being self-taught in the art of riding, grooms nearly always have a very heavy bridle hand, and, if allowed to use the curb bit, will soon destroy that sensitiveness of the horse's mouth which adds so much to the pleasure of riding him. The man who exercises the horse should not be permitted to wear spurs; a lady's horse should be guided wholly by the whip and reins,—as will be explained hereafter,—and in no case whatever should the spur be used. If the lady wishes to keep her horse in good health and temper she must insist upon his being exercised regularly, and must assure herself that the groom executes her orders faithfully; for some men, while professing to obey, have been known to stop at the nearest public house, and, after spending an hour or two in drinking beer and gossiping with acquaintances, to ride back complacently to the stable, leaving the horse to suffer from want of exercise. Other grooms have gone to the opposite extreme, and have ridden so hard and fast that the horse on his[51] return was completely tired out, so that when there was occasion to use him the same day it was an effort for him to maintain his usual light gait. Grooms who are always doctoring a horse, giving him nostrums that do no good but often much harm, are also to be avoided. In short, the owner of a horse must be prepared for tricks of all kinds on the part of these stable servants; although, in justice to them, it must be said that there are many who endeavor to perform all their duties faithfully, and can be relied on to treat with kindness any animals committed to their care.

Should the lady rider be obliged to get her horse from a livery stable, she should not rely entirely upon what his owner says of his gaits or gentleness, but should have him tried carefully by some friend or servant, before herself attempting to mount him. She should also be very careful to see, or have her escort see, that the saddle is properly placed upon the back of the horse and firmly girthed, so that there may be no danger of its turning.

[52]

CHAPTER II.
THE RIDING HABIT.

"Her dress, her shape, her matchless grace,
Were all observed, as well as heavenly face."

DRYDEN.

A riding habit should be distinguished by its perfect simplicity. All attempts at display, such as feathers, ribbons, glaring gilt buttons, and sparkling jet, should be carefully avoided, and the dress should be noticeable only for the fineness of its material and the elegance of its fit.

One of the first requirements in a riding dress is that it should fit smoothly and easily. The sleeves should be rather loose, especially near the arm-holes, so that the arms may move freely; but should fit closely enough at the wrist to allow long gauntlet gloves to pass readily over them. It is essential that ample room should be allowed across the chest, as the shoulders are thrown somewhat back in riding, and the chest is, consequently, expanded. The neck of the dress should fit very easily, especially at the back part. Care must be taken not to make the waist too long, for, owing to a[53] lady's position in the saddle, the movements of her horse will soon make a long waist wrinkle and look inelegant. To secure ease, together with a perfect fit without crease or fold, will be somewhat difficult, but not impossible. Some tailors, particularly in New York, Philadelphia, London, and Paris, make a specialty of ladies' riding costumes, and can generally be relied on to supply comfortable and elegant habits.

The favorite and most appropriate style of **riding jacket** is the "postilion basque;" this should be cut short over the hips, and is then especially becoming to a plump person, as it diminishes the apparent width of the back below the waist. The front should have two small darts, and should extend about three inches below the waist; it should then slope gradually up to the hips,—where it must be shortest,—and then downward so as to form a short, square coat-flap at the back, below the waist. This flap must be made without gathers or plaits, and lined with silk, between which and the cloth some stiffening material should be inserted. The middle seam of the coat-flap should be left open as far as the waist, where about one inch of it must be lapped over from left to right; the short side-form on each side must be lapped a little toward the central unclosed[54] seam. The arm-holes should be cut rather high on the shoulders, so that the back may look less broad. If the lady lacks plumpness and roundness, her jacket must be made double-breasted, or else have padding placed across the bust, for a hollow chest mars all the beauty of the figure in the saddle, and causes the rider to look round-shouldered. The edge of the basque should be trimmed with cord-braid, and the front fastened with crocheted bullet buttons; similar buttons should be used to fasten the sleeves closely at the wrist, and two more should be placed on the back of the basque just at its waist line.

Great care must be taken to have the jacket well lined and its seams strongly sewed. The coat-flaps on the back of the basque, below the waist-line, should be held down by heavy metallic buttons, sewed underneath each flap at its lower part, and covered with the same material as that of the dress. Without these weights this part of the dress will be apt to be blown out of position by every passing breeze, and will bob up and down with every motion of the rider's body, presenting a most ridiculous appearance.

For winter riding an extra jacket may be worn over the riding basque. It should be made of some heavy, warm material, and fit half[55] tightly. If trimmed with good fur, this jacket makes a very handsome addition to the riding habit.

Poets have expatiated upon the grace and beauty of the long, flowing riding skirt, with its ample folds, but experience has taught that this long skirt, though, perhaps, very poetical, is practically not only inconvenient but positively dangerous. In the canter or gallop the horse is very apt to entangle his hind-foot in it and be thrown, when the rider may consider herself fortunate if she escapes with no worse accident than a torn skirt. Another objection to this poetical skirt is, that it gathers up the mud and dust of the road, and soon presents a most untidy appearance; while if the day be fresh and breezy its ample folds will stream out like a victorious banner; if made of some light material the breeze will swell it out like an inflated balloon; and if of heavy cloth its length will envelop the rider's feet, and make her look as if tied in a bag.

To avoid all these dangers and inconveniences the **riding skirt** should be cut rather short and narrow, and be made of some heavy material. Two yards and a quarter will be quite wide enough for the bottom of the skirt, while the length need be only about twelve inches more[56] than the rider's ordinary dress. The skirt should be so gored as to form no gathers or plaits at the waist. Tailor-made skirts are so neatly gored as to remain perfectly smooth when the rider is seated in the saddle. As the pommels take up a good deal of room, the front part of the skirt, which passes over them, should be made a little longer than the back, so that, when the rider is seated in the saddle, her dress may hang evenly. If made the same length all around it will, when the lady is mounted, be entirely too short in front, and, besides presenting an uneven, trail-like appearance, will be apt to work back, or to blow up and expose the right foot of the wearer.

The bottom of the skirt should have a hem about three inches wide, but should never be faced with leather, as this will give a stiff, bungling effect, and if the rider should be thrown, and catch the hem of her skirt on either pommel or stirrup, the strength of the leather lining would prevent the cloth from tearing and thus releasing her. Shot, pieces of lead, or other hard substances are also objectionable, because by striking against the horse's side they often cause him to become restless or even to run away. To keep the skirt down in its proper position a loop of stout elastic, or tape, should[57] be fastened underneath, near the bottom, and through this loop the foot should be passed before being put into the stirrup. The point where the loop should be fastened must be determined by the position of the lady's foot when she is correctly seated in the saddle. Some riders use a second elastic for the right foot, to prevent the skirt from slipping back, but this is not absolutely necessary.

The basque and skirt should be made separate, although it is a very good plan to have strong hooks and eyes to fasten them together at the sides and back, as this will prevent the skirt from turning, or slipping down below the waist, should the binding be a little too loose. The placket-hole should be on the left side and should be buttoned over, to prevent it from gaping open; it must be only just large enough to allow the skirt to slip readily over the shoulders.

The best material for a riding habit is broadcloth, or any strong, soft fabric that will adapt itself readily to the figure. The color is, of course, a matter of taste. Black is always stylish, and is particularly becoming to a stout person. Dark blue, hunter's green, and dark brown are also becoming colors, especially for slender, youthful figures. In the country, a linen[58] jacket may be worn in warm weather, and will be found a very agreeable substitute for the cloth basque, but the skirt should never be made of so thin a material, as it will be too light to hang well and too slippery to sit upon.

To secure ease and freedom in the saddle, a garment closely resembling a pair of**pantaloons** will have to be worn under the riding skirt, and be fastened down securely by means of strong leather or rubber straps, which pass under the foot and are buttoned to the bottom of the pantaloons. These pantaloons should be made of some soft cloth the color of the dress, or else of chamois skin, faced up to the knee with cloth like that of the skirt. Most people prefer the chamois skin for winter use, as it is very warm and so soft that it prevents much of the chafing usually occasioned by the rubbing of the right leg on the pommel.

No under **petticoats** are necessary where the pantaloons are used, but if the rider wear one, it should be of some dark color that will not attract attention if the riding skirt be blown back. Black silk will be an excellent material for such a skirt in summer, something warmer being used in winter. This skirt should have no folds or gathers in it, but if the rider be very thin a little padding around the hips and over the[59] back will give her the desired effect of plumpness.

An important article of every-day wear will have to be discarded and a **riding-habit shirt** used in its place. This shirt must be made short, that the rider may not have to sit upon its folds and wrinkles, which she would find very uncomfortable. The collar should be high and standing, *à la militaire*, and made of the finest, whitest linen; it should be sewed to the shirt for greater security, and should just be seen above the high collar band of the basque.

The **drawers** must also be made very much like those of a gentleman, and the lower parts be tucked under the hose. The garters should be rather loose, or elastic.

Buttoned boots, or those with elastic sides, should not be worn when riding. For summer use, the shoe laced at the side, and having a low, broad heel, is liked by many. The ladies' Wellington boot, reaching nearly to the knee, is also a favorite with some, and, when made without any seam in front, prevents the stirrup-iron from chafing the instep. To be comfortable, it should have a broad sole and be made a little longer than the foot. This boot, however, gives the wearer rather an Amazonian appearance, and has also the great disadvantage of being[60] very difficult to get off, the lady usually being obliged to appropriate the gentleman's bootjack for the purpose. The **best boot** for riding purposes, found to be the most comfortable, and one easy to get on and off, is made of some light leather, or kid, for summer use, and of heavier leather for winter; it extends half way to the knee, laces up in front, has broad, low heels and wide soles, and is made a little longer than the wearer's foot, so that it may be perfectly easy, as a tight boot in riding is even more distressing than in walking.

The **corset** is indispensable to the elegant fit required in a riding habit, but should never be laced tight. It should be short on the sides and in the front and back. If long in front it will be almost impossible for the rider to pass her knee over the second pommel when she attempts to mount her horse, and will cause her, when riding, to incline her body too far back; when long at the sides it will be even more inconvenient, for, if at all tight, it will make the rider, when in the saddle, feel as if her hips were compressed in a vise; when too long behind, it will interfere with that curving or hollowing in of the back that is so necessary to an erect position; it will also tend to throw the body too far forward. If the rider have any tendency to[61] stoutness all these discomforts will be exaggerated. The C. P. or the Parisian *la Sirene*is undoubtedly the best corset for riding purposes, for it is short, light, and flexible, and not prejudicial to the ease and elegance of good riding, as is the case with the stiff, long-bodied corset.

The **hair** should be so arranged that it cannot possibly come down during the ride. To effect this, it must be made into one long braid, which must be coiled upon the back of the head, and fastened firmly, but not too tightly, by means of a few long hairpins. The coil may be put on the top of the head, but this arrangement will be found very inconvenient, especially where the hair is thick, for it will make the hat sit very awkwardly on the head. The hair should never be worn in ringlets, as these will be blown about by the wind, or by the movements of the rider, and will soon become so tangled as to look like anything but the "smooth flowing ringlets" of the poet. Nor should the hair be allowed to stream down the back in long peasant-braids, a style mistakenly adopted by some young misses, but which gives the rider a wild and untidy appearance. When the horse is in motion these braids will stream out on the breeze, and an observer at a short distance will be puzzled to know what it is that seems to be[62] in such an extraordinary state of agitation. It is also a mistake to draw the hair back tightly from the forehead, as this gives a constrained look to the features; it should, on the contrary, be arranged in rather a loose, unstudied manner, which will tend to soften the expression of the face. It is the extreme of bad taste to bang or frizz the hair across the forehead, or to wear the hat somewhat on the back of the head. These things are sometimes done by very young girls, but give to the prettiest and most modest face an air of boldness and vulgarity.

The **riding hat** at present fashionable, and most suitable for city or park, is made of black silk plush with a Stanley curved brim, and bell-crown, and is trimmed with a narrow band around the crown, directly above the brim. Another favorite is a jockey-cap, made of the same cloth as that of the habit. Either of these may be obtained at the hat stores. For riding in the country, where one does not care to be so dressy, the English Derby, or some other fashionable style of young gentleman's felt hat, may be used; with a short plume or bird's wing fastened at the side, a hat of this description has a very charming and coquettish air. There is another style of silk hat manufactured expressly for ladies, which may also be obtained at[63] any hatter's; it has a lower crown than a gentleman's silk hat, and looks very pretty with a short black net-veil fastened around the crown, as this relieves the stiff look it otherwise presents. This style of hat is very appropriate for a middle-aged person. Care must be taken to have the hat neither too loose nor too tight; if too tight, it will be apt to occasion a headache, and if too loose will be easily displaced.

Long veils, long plumes, hats with very broad brims, or very high crowns, as well as those which are worn perched on the top of the head, should be especially avoided. The hat must always be made secure on the head by means of stout elastic sewn on strongly, and so adjusted that it can pass below the braid or coil of hair at the back of the head. An ordinary back-comb firmly fastened on the top of the head will prevent the hat from gradually slipping backwards.

These apparently trifling details must be attended to, or some prankish breeze will suddenly carry off the rider's hat, and she will be subjected to the mortification of having it handed back to her, with an ill-concealed smile, by some obliging pedestrian. Many little particulars which seem insignificant when in the dressing-room will become causes of much discomfort and[64] suffering when in the saddle. The pleasure of many a ride has been marred by a displaced pin, a lost button, too tight a garter, a glove that cramped the hand, or a ring that occasioned swelling and pain in the finger. These details, unimportant as they may seem, must be carefully attended to before starting for a ride. Pins should be used sparingly. If a watch is worn, it should be well secured in its pocket, and the chain carefully fastened to a button of the jacket.

The **riding gauntlets** should be made of thick, soft, undressed kid, or chamois skin, be long wristed, and somewhat loose across the hands, so that the reins may be firmly grasped. With the exception of the watch, the chain of which should be as unostentatious as possible, it will not be in good taste to wear jewelry. A cravat or small bow of ribbon will be in much better taste than a breast-pin for fastening the collar, and may be of any color that suits the fancy or complexion of the wearer. The costume may be much brightened by a small *boutonnière* of natural flowers; these placed at the throat or waist in an apparently careless manner give an air of daintiness and refinement to the whole costume.

There is one accomplishment often neglected,[65] or overlooked, even by the most skillful lady riders, and that is, expertness in **holding the riding skirt** easily and gracefully when not in the saddle. In this attainment the Parisian horsewoman far excels all others; her manner of gathering up the folds of her riding skirt, while waiting for her horse, forms a picture of such unaffected elegance, that it would be well for other riders to study and imitate it. She does not grab her skirt with one hand, twist it round to one side, allow it to trail upon the ground, nor does she collect the folds in one unwieldy bunch and throw it brusquely over her arm. Instead of any of these ungraceful acts, she quietly extends her arms down to their full length at her sides, inclines her body slightly forward, and gathers up the front of her skirt, raising her hands just far enough to allow the long part in front and at the sides to escape the ground; then by bringing her hands slightly forward, one being held a little higher than the other, the back part of the skirt is raised. While accomplishing these movements her whip will be held carelessly in her right hand, at a very short distance below the handle, the point being directed downwards, and somewhat obliquely backwards. The whole of this graceful manœuvring will be effected readily and artlessly,[66] in an apparently unstudied manner. In reality, however, all the Parisian's ease and grace are the results of careful training, but so perfect is the instruction that art is made to appear like nature.

In selecting a **riding whip** care should be taken to secure one that is straight and stiff; if it be curved, it may accidentally touch the horse and make him restless; if flexible it will be of no use in managing him. The handle of the whip may be very plain, or the lady may indulge her taste for the ornamental by having it very elaborate and rich, but she should be careful never to sacrifice strength to appearances. Any projecting points that might catch on the dress and tear it must be dispensed with. That the whip may not be lost if the hand should unwittingly lose its hold upon it, a loop of silk cord should be fastened firmly to the handle, and the hand passed through this loop. When riding, the whip should always be held in the right hand with a grasp sufficient to retain it, but not as if in a vise; the point should be directed downward, or toward the hind-leg of the horse, care being taken not to touch him with it except when necessary.

[67]

CHAPTER III.
THE SADDLE AND BRIDLE.

"Form by mild bits his mouth, nor harshly wound,
Till summer rolls her fourth-revolving round.
Then wheel in graceful orbs his paced career,
Let step by step in cadence strike the ear,
The flexile limbs in curves alternate prance,
And seem to labor as they slow advance:
Then give, uncheck'd, to fly with loosen'd rein,
Challenge the winds, and wing th' unprinted plain."

VIRGIL, *Sotheby's Translation.*

In ye ancient times, the damsel who wished to enjoy horseback riding did not, like her successor of to-day, trust to her own ability to ride and manage her horse, but, seated upon a pad or cushion, called a "pillion," which was fastened behind a man's saddle, rode without a stirrup and without troubling herself with the reins, preserving her balance by holding to the belt of a trusty page, or masculine admirer, whose duty it was to attend to the management of the horse. We learn that as late as A. D. 1700, George III. made his entry into London with his wife, Charlotte, thus seated behind him. Gradually, however, as women became more confident, they rode alone upon a sort of side-saddle,[68] on which by means of the reins and by bracing her feet against a board, called a "planchette," which was fastened to the front of the saddle, the rider managed to keep her seat. Such was the English horsewoman of the seventeenth century, in the time of Charles II.,—"the height of fashion and the cream of style."

To the much quoted "vanity of the fair sex" do we owe the invention of the side-saddle of our grandmothers. About the middle of the sixteenth century Catherine de Medici, wife of Henry II. of France, having a very symmetrical figure which she wished to display to advantage, invented the second pommel of the saddle, and thus, while gratifying her own vanity, was unconsciously the means of greatly benefiting her sex by enabling them to ride with more ease and freedom. To this saddle there was added, about 1830, a third pommel, the invention of which is due to the late M.

Pellier, Sr., an eminent riding teacher in Paris, France. This three-pommeled saddle is now called the **English saddle**, and is the one generally used by the best lady riders of the present day.

This so-called "English saddle" was promptly appreciated, and wherever introduced soon supplanted the old-fashioned one with only two pommels. (Fig. 7.)

[69]

Fig. 7.—English Saddle.

1, second pommel; 2, third pommel; 3, shield; 4, saddle-flap; 5, cantle; 6, stirrup-leather; 7, stirrup; 8, girths; 9, platform.

View larger image.

A lady who has once ridden one of these three-pommeled saddles will never care to use any other kind. It renders horseback riding almost perfectly safe, for, if the rider has learned to use it properly, it will be nearly impossible for a horse to throw her. It gives her a much firmer seat even than that of a gentleman in his saddle, and at the same time, if rightly used, does not interfere with that easy grace so essential to good riding. In many of our large cities where this saddle is employed twenty lady riders may now be seen in the park or on the road where formerly there was one; and this is [70] wholly due to the sense of security it gives, especially to a timid rider, a feeling never attainable in the two-pommeled saddle, where the seat is maintained chiefly by the balance, or by using the reins as a means of support.

By sitting erect, taking a firm hold upon the second pommel with the right knee, and pressing the left knee up against the third pommel, a perfectly secure seat is obtained, from which the rider cannot be shaken, provided the saddle is well girthed and the horse does not fall, while her hands are left free to manage the reins, a very important point where the horse is spirited or restless. To insure the greatest safety and comfort for both horse and rider, it is very important that the saddle should be accurately constructed. If possible, it should be made especially for the horse that is to carry it, so that it may suit his particular shape. If it does not fit him well, it will be likely to turn, or may gall his back severely, and make him for a long time unfit for service. It may even, in time, give rise to fistulous withers, will certainly make the horse restless and uneasy on the road, and the pain he suffers will interfere with the ease and harmony of his gaits. Many a horse has been rendered unfit for a lady's use solely because the saddle did not fit well.

[71]

The under surface of the arch of the saddle-tree, in front, should never come in contact with the animal's withers, nor should the points of the saddle-tree be so tightly fitted as to interfere with the movements of his shoulders. On the other hand, they should not be so far apart as to allow the central furrowed line of the under surface of the saddle (the chamber) to rest upon the animal's back. The saddle should be so fitted and padded that this central chamber will lie directly over the spinal column of the horse without touching it, while the padded surfaces, just below the chamber, should rest closely on the sides of the back, and be supported at as many points as is possible without making the animal uncomfortable.

When a horse has very high withers, a breast-plate, similar to that employed in military service, may be used, to prevent the saddle from slipping backwards. This contrivance consists of a piece of leather passing round the neck like a collar, to the lowest part of which is fastened a strap that passes between the fore-legs of the horse and is attached to the saddle girth. Two other straps, one on each side, connect the upper part of the collar piece with the upper part of the saddle. The under strap should never be very loose, for should the saddle slip [72] back and this strap not be tight enough to hold down the collar piece, the latter will be pulled up by the upper straps so as to press against the windpipe of the horse and choke him. Should the horse have low withers and a round, barrel-like body, false pannels or padded pieces may be used; but an animal of this shape is not suitable for a lady, for it will be almost impossible to keep the saddle from turning, no matter how carefully it may be girthed.

A sufficiently spacious seat or platform to the saddle is much more comfortable for both horse and rider than a narrow one. It gives the rider a firmer seat, and does not bring so much strain upon the girths. This platform should also be made as nearly level as possible, and be covered with quilted buckskin. Leather, now so often used for this purpose, becomes after a time so slippery that it is difficult to retain one's seat, and the pommels when covered with it are apt to chafe the limbs severely.

To secure a thoroughly comfortable saddle it is necessary that not only the horse, but also the rider, should be measured for it; for a saddle suitable for a slender person could hardly be used with any comfort by a stout one, and it is almost as bad to have a saddle too large as too small. Care must be taken to have sufficient[73] length from the front of the second pommel to the cantle. In the ready-made saddles this distance is usually too short, and the rider is obliged to sit upon the back edge of the seat, thereby injuring both herself and her horse. It is much better to err in the other direction and have the seat too long rather than too short. The third pommel should be so placed that it will just span the knee when the stirrup-leather is of the right length. It should be rather short, slightly curved, and blunt. If it be too long and have too much of a curve, it will, in the English trot, interfere with the free action of the rider's left leg, and if the horse should fall, it would be almost impossible for her to disengage her leg and free herself in time to escape injury. The third pommel must be so placed as not to interfere with the position of the right leg when this is placed around the second pommel with the right heel drawn backwards. To get the proper proportions for her saddle, the lady must, when seated, take her measure from the under side of the knee joint to the lower extremity of her back, and also—to secure the proper width for the seat—from thigh to thigh. If these two measurements are given to the saddle-maker he will, if he understands his business, be able to construct the saddle properly.

[74]

The saddle recommended by the author, one which she has used for several years, and still continues to use, is represented in Fig. 7. The third pommel of this saddle is of medium size, and instead of being close to the second one is placed a short distance below it, thus enabling the rider to use a longer stirrup than she otherwise could; for if the two pommels be very close together, the rider will be obliged to use a very short stirrup in order to make this third pommel of any use. The disadvantage of a short stirrup is that, in a long ride, it is apt to occasion cramp in the left leg. It also interferes with an easy and steady position in the saddle. But with a stirrup of the right length, and the arrangement of the pommels such as we have described, a steadiness is given to the left leg that can never be obtained with the old-fashioned two-pommeled saddle.

The third pommel must be screwed securely into the saddle-tree, and once fixed in its proper place, should not again be moved, as if frequently turned it will soon get loose, and the rider will not be able to rely upon its assistance to retain her balance. It should be screwed into place inversely, that is, instead of being turned to the right it must be turned to the left, so that the pressure of the knee may make it[75] firmer and more secure, instead of loosening it, as would be the case if it were screwed to the right. This pommel should be well padded, so that the knee may not be bruised by it.

The second pommel should also be well padded, and should always be curved slightly so as to suit the form of the right leg. It must not be so high as to render it difficult, in mounting and dismounting, to pass the right knee over it. The off-pommel, since the English saddle has come into vogue, has almost disappeared, being reduced to a mere vestige of its former size. This is a great improvement to the rider's appearance, as she now no longer has that confined, cribbed-up look which the high pommeled saddle of twenty years ago gave her.

The distance between the off-pommel and the second one should be adapted to the size of the rider's leg, being wide enough to allow the leg to rest easily between the two; but no wider than this, as too much space will be apt to lead her to sit sideways upon the saddle.

A saddle should be well padded, but not so much so as to lift the rider too high above the horse's back. The shield in front should not press upon the neck of the horse, but should barely touch it. The saddle flaps must be well strapped down, for if they stand out stiffly, the[76] correct position of the stirrup leg will be interfered with. A side-saddle should never be too light in weight, for this will make the back of the horse sore, especially if he be ridden by a heavy woman.

The tacks or nails in the under part of the saddle should be firmly driven in, as they may otherwise become loose and either injure the horse, or make him nervous and uneasy. To avoid trouble of this kind, some people advocate the use of false pannels, which are fastened to the saddle-tree by rods or loops, and can be removed and replaced at will. It is said that by using them, the same saddle can be made to fit different horses. The author has no personal knowledge of this invention, but it has been strongly recommended to her by several excellent horsemen. A felt or flannel saddle cloth, of the same color as the rider's habit, should always be placed under the saddle, as it helps to protect the horse's back, as well as to prevent the saddle from getting soiled.

Every finished side-saddle has three girths. Two of these are made of felt cloth, or strong webbing, and are designed to fasten it firmly upon the horse's back. The third one, made of leather, is intended to keep the flaps down. There should always be, on each side, three [77] straps fastened to the saddle-tree under the leather flaps; upon two of these the girths are to be buckled, while the third is an extra one, to be used as a substitute in case of any accident to either of the others. Between the outside leather flaps and the horse's body there should be an under flap of flannel or cloth, which should be well padded on the side next the horse, because, when tightly girthed, the girth-buckles press directly upon the outside of this flap, and if its padding be thin, or worn, the animal will suffer great pain. This is a cause of restlessness which is seldom noticed, and many a horse has been thought to be bad tempered when he was only wild with pain from [78] the pressure of the girth-buckles against his side.

Fig. 8.—Stokes' mode of girthing the saddle.

The credit of introducing a new method of tightening girths belongs, so far as we know, to Mr. Stokes, formerly a riding-teacher in Cincinnati. This method enables one to girth the horse tightly, without using so much muscular effort as is usually required, so that by its means, a lady can, if she wish, saddle her own horse. (Fig. 8.)

The following is a description of Mr. Stokes' manner of girthing: At the end of each of the leather girth straps, which hang down between the flaps on the off-side of the saddle, is fastened a strong iron buckle without any tongue, but with a thin steel roller or revolving cylinder on its lower edge. On the near side of the saddle the girths are strapped in the usual manner, but, on the *outer* end of each cloth girth there is, in addition to an ordinary buckle, with a roller on the upper side of it, a long strap, which is fastened to the under side of the girth, the buckle being on the upper side. This strap, when the saddle is girthed, is passed up through the tongueless buckle, moving easily over the steel roller, and is then brought down to the buckle with tongue on the end of the girth, and there fastened in the usual manner.

[79]

The slipper stirrup, when first introduced, was a great favorite, for in addition to furnishing an excellent support, it was believed that it would release the foot instantly should the rider be thrown. This latter merit, however, it was found that it did not possess, as many severe accidents occurred where this stirrup was used, especially with the two-pommeled saddle. Instead of releasing the rider in these cases, as it was supposed it would, the stirrup tilted up and held her foot so firmly grasped that she was dragged some distance before she could be released. This stirrup, therefore, gradually fell into disfavor, and is now no longer used by the best riders.

Fig. 9.—Victoria stirrup.

There are, at the present time, three kinds of stirrups which are favorites among finished riders. The first is called the "Victoria" because [80] it is the one used by the Queen of England. (Fig. 9.) In this stirrup the platform on which the foot rests is broad and comfortable, and is slightly roughened to prevent the foot from slipping. A spring-bar attachment (Fig. 10) is placed at the top of the stirrup-leather under the saddle-flap, and at the end of this bar there is a spring, so that, if the rider be thrown, the stirrup-leather becomes instantly detached from the saddle.

Fig. 10.—Spring-bar for stirrup leather.

The second variety of stirrup, known as "Lennan's safety stirrup," has all the merit of the preceding one. If kept well oiled and free from mud, it will release the foot at once, when an accident occurs. It may, if desired, be accompanied by the spring-bar attachment, and thus rendered doubly secure. (Fig. 11.) Some people, however, dislike the spring-bar attachment, and prefer to rely entirely upon the spring of the stirrup to release the foot.

Fig. 11.—Lennan's safety stirrup.

The third stirrup, called "Latchford's safety stirrup," consists of a stirrup within a stirrup, [81] and is so arranged that, when a rider is thrown, the inner stirrup springs open and releases the foot. (Fig. 12.) Either of these stirrups can be procured in London, England, or from the best saddle-makers in this country.

Fig. 12.—Latchford's safety stirrup.

A **stirrup-iron** should never be made of cast metal, but invariably of the best wrought steel: it should be adapted to the size of the rider's foot, and should, if possible, have an instep pad at the top, while the bottom platform, upon which the foot rests, should be broad, and roughened on its upper surface.

The **stirrup-leather** should be of the very best material, and should have neither fissures nor cracks in any part of it. It is very important to examine this leather frequently, and see that it is neither wearing thin, nor breaking at its upper part at the bar, nor at the lower part where it is fastened to the stirrup.

A novel arrangement of the stirrup-leather, by means of the so-called "balance-strap," has of late years been used by some riders. The stirrup is, in this case, fastened to the balance-strap, which consists of a single strap passing up [82] through the ring-bar, and then brought down to within two or three inches of the lower edge of the saddle-flap; here it is passed through a slit in the flap, then carried under the horse to the other side and buckled to another strap, which is fastened, for this purpose, just below the off-pommel. By this arrangement the saddle-flaps on both sides are held down, and the rider, without dismounting, can change the length of her stirrup by merely tightening or loosening this strap. Although highly recommended by some riders, this balance strap has one objectionable feature, which is that, as the measurement of the horse's girth is not constant during a long ride, it will be necessary to tighten the strap frequently in order to keep the stirrup of the proper length. The old way of fastening is much better, for too much complication in the saddle and bridle is apt to annoy and confuse the rider, especially if a novice. The **golden rule** in riding on horseback is to have everything accurate, simple, safe, and made of the very best material that can be procured.

The **bridle** should be neatly and plainly made, with no large rosettes at the sides, nor highly colored bands across the forehead. The reins and the head-piece should never be made [83] of rounded straps, but always of flat ones, and should be of the best and strongest leather, especially the reins. These should be carefully examined from time to time, in order to be sure that there are no imperfections in them. Any roughness or hardness is an indication of defectiveness, and may be detected by dexterously passing the fingers to and fro over the flat surfaces, which should be smooth, soft, and flexible. There can hardly be too much care taken about this matter, for the snapping of a rein always alarms a horse; and, feeling himself free from all control, he will be almost certain to run away, while the rider, if she has no other reins, will be powerless to protect herself, or to check him in his purpose.

Martingales are rarely used by riders, as they are troublesome, and can very well be dispensed with, unless the horse has the disagreeable trick of raising his head suddenly, from time to time, when a martingale will become necessary in order to correct this fault. The French martingale is the best. This consists of a single strap, fastened either to the under part of a nose-band at its centre under the jaw, or by branches to each side of the snaffle-bit at the corners of the horse's mouth and then carried between the fore-legs and fastened to the girth. [84] When the horse raises his head too high this strap pulls upon the nose-band, compresses his nostrils, interferes with his breathing, and causes him to lower his head promptly. The horse should not be too much confined by the martingale, for the object is simply to prevent him from lifting his head too high, and all other ordinary movements should be left free.

Fig. 13.—Chifney bit.

Among the many **bits** which have been used, that known as the "Pelham" has been highly praised, although, at the present time, it is almost, if not entirely, out of use. It might, however, from the severity of its curb prove of service in controlling a hard-mouthed horse, although such a one should never be ridden by a lady. The Chifney bit is another very severe one, and is very useful in managing a horse that pulls hard. But if the animal have a tender mouth, this bit should be used with great caution, and not at all by an inexperienced rider. (Fig. 13.)

The bit known as the "snaffle," when made plain and not twisted, is the mildest of all bits, and some horses will move readily only when[85] this is used, the curb instantly rousing their temper. Others, again, do best with a combination of the curb and the snaffle, and although the former may seldom require to be used, its mere presence in the mouth of the horse will prove a sufficient check to prevent him from running away. Most horses, however, especially those ridden by ladies, require a light use of the curb to bring them to their best gait.

Fig. 14.—The Combination Bit.

***a*, *a*, rings fastened on each side to small bar, at right angles to and directed backward of the cheek; *b*, *b*, rings for the curb-reins.**

View larger image.

The bit used and recommended by many, but not by the author, is a curb so arranged as to form a combination bit in one piece. It consists of a curb (Fig. 14), to each side of which, at the angles of the horse's mouth, a ring is attached, and to each of these rings is fastened a rein. This gives a second pair of reins and converts the curb into a kind of snaffle. In this way it answers the purpose of both curb and snaffle without crowding the horse's mouth with two separate bits.

If two bits should be used—the curb and bridoon—instead of the above combination bit, the bridoon should be placed in the horse's[86] mouth in such a way as not to interfere with the action of the curb; it must, therefore, be neither too thick nor too long, and so fitted into the angles of the mouth as to neither wrinkle nor draw back the lips.

The bit should always be made of the best steel, be well rounded, and perfectly smooth. Above all it should be accurately fitted to the horse's mouth: if it be too narrow it will compress his lips against the bars of his mouth, and the pain thereby occasioned will render him very restive. The mouth-piece should be just long enough to have the cheeks of the bit fit closely to the outer surface of the lips without compressing them, and must not be so long as to become displaced obliquely when a rein is pulled.

Fig. 15.—Dwyer's Curb-Bit.

1, 1, upper bars or cheeks; 2, 2, lower bars; 3, the port; 4, 4, the canons; 5, curb-chain; 6, curb-hook; 7, lip strap and ring; 8, 8, rein rings; 9, 9, head stall rings.

View larger image.

According to Major Dwyer, who is a high authority on the subject of bits,—and whose little work should be carefully studied by all bit-makers,—it seems to be the general rule to have the lower bar or cheek of the curb-bit twice as long as the upper one; but, as there is no standard measure[87] for the upper one the other is frequently made too long. Major Dwyer states that the mouth-piece, for any horse of ordinary size, should be one and three fourths inches for the upper bar, and three and a half inches for the lower one. This makes five and one fourth inches for the entire length of the two bars, from the point at which the curb-hook acts above to that where the lower ring acts below. (Fig. 15.) For ordinary ponies the upper bar may be one and a half inches, and the lower one three, making a total length of four and a half inches.

Every lady rider should know that the longer the lower bar, the thinner the mouth-piece, and the higher the "port," the more severe and painful will be the action of the bit upon the horse's mouth. For a horse of ordinary size, the width of the port should be one and one third inches; for a pony, one inch. The height will vary according to the degree of severity required.

The curb-chain, for a horse that has a chin-groove of medium size, should be about four fifths of an inch wide, as a chain that is rather broad and flat is less painful for the horse than a thin, sharp one. If the chin-groove be very narrow, a curb-chain of less width will have to[88] be used, and should be covered with cloth; or, instead of a chain, a narrow strap of leather may be used, which should be kept soft and pliable. The proper length for the curb-chain, not including the curb-hooks, is about one fourth more than the width of the animal's mouth. The hooks should be exactly alike, and about an inch and a quarter long.

Some horses are very expert in the trick of catching the cheek of the bit between their teeth. To remedy this vice a lip-strap may be used; but it will be found much better to have each cheek or bar bent into the form of the letter S, remembering, however, that the measurement of the length, referred to above, must in the case of curved bars be made in a straight line. Sometimes the upper bar of the curb-bit will, on account of the peculiar form of the horse's head, press against and gall his cheeks. When this is noticed, most people change the bit, and get one with a longer mouth-piece; but where the mouth-piece is of the same length as the width of the mouth, the proper remedy for this difficulty will be to have the upper bar bent out enough to free the cheeks from its pressure.

The curb-bit once made and properly adjusted to the head-stall, the next step will be to[89] **fit it accurately** to the horse's mouth. Every rider should thoroughly understand not only how to do this, but also how to place the saddle correctly upon the horse. Upon these points nearly all grooms require instruction, and very few gentlemen, even, know how to arrange a side-saddle so as to have it comfortable for both horse and rider. Moreover, should the lady be riding alone, as frequently happens in the country, and meet with any accident to saddle or bridle, or need to have either adjusted, she would, without knowledge on these subjects, be completely helpless, whereas with it she could promptly remedy the difficulty.

Fig. 16.—The Bit adjusted.
1, 1, snaffle-rein; 2, 2, curb-rein.
View larger image.

In order to adjust the bit permanently to the head-stall, so that afterwards the horse can always be properly bridled, one must proceed as follows: having first fitted the head-stall to the horse's head by means of the upper buckles, the bit must then be adjusted, by means of the lower ones, in such a manner that the canons of the mouth-piece will rest on the bars of the horse's mouth, exactly opposite the chin-groove. (Fig. 16.) Should the tusks of the horse be irregularly placed, the mouth-piece must be adjusted a little higher than the projecting tusks, so as to just avoid touching them. The curb-chain may now be hooked into the ring of the upper[90] bar on the off-side, leaving one link loose, after which the other hook must be fastened to the ring of the bar on the near-side, leaving two links loose. Care should be taken to have the curb-chain rest with its flat surface against the chin-groove in such a way that it will have no tendency to rise up when the reins are pulled upon. The curb-chain should never be tight; there must always be room enough between it and the chin to insert the first and second fingers of the right hand flatwise; and, while the fingers are thus placed, if the reins are drawn[91] up, it will be easy to ascertain whether the chain pinches. If, when the reins are tightened, the bit stands stiff and immovable, it will show that the chain is too short and needs to be lengthened a link or two. If the horse gently yields his head to the tightening of the reins, without suddenly drawing back, or thrusting out his nose as the tension is increased, it will prove that the bit is correctly placed. But if the lower bars of the bit can be drawn back quite a distance before the horse will yield to the pull of the reins, then the chain is too long, and should be shortened. "Lightness, accuracy, easy motion, a total absence of stiffness, constraint, or painful action, are the characteristics of good bitting; and if these be attained, ready obedience to the rider's hand will be the result."—*F. Dwyer.*

When the bit has once been correctly adjusted to the head-stall and to the horse's mouth, there will be little difficulty in bridling him upon any subsequent occasion. Thus: standing at the left of the horse's head, the head-stall, held by its upper part in the right hand, should be lifted up in front of the horse's head, while the left hand, holding the bit by its mouth-piece, should put this between the animal's lips, press it against his teeth, and into his[92] mouth, which he will generally open a little in order to admit it. As soon as this has been accomplished, the upper part of the head-stall must be promptly raised so as to bring its upper strap or band across the forehead, while at the same time the horse's ears are passed between the forehead band and the strap which forms the upper part of the head-stall.

During these manœuvres, the curb-chain must be passed under the chin, so as to rest against the chin-groove, and care be taken to keep the fingers of the left hand out of the horse's mouth while the mouth-piece is being put in. The bit and head-stall having been properly arranged, the whole should be secured by buckling the throat-strap loosely on the left side. If this strap be buckled tightly, the horse will be unable to bend his neck properly. The mouth-piece of the bit should be washed, dried, and then rubbed with fresh olive or cotton-seed oil, each time after use, to preserve it from rust.

Neither a rusted bit nor a very cold one should ever be put into a horse's mouth. In frosty winter weather the bit should always be warmed. Many a valuable horse has had his mouth seriously injured by having an icy cold mouth-piece put into it, to say nothing of the pain and suffering it must invariably occasion.

[93]

In order to produce a neat and pleasing appearance, there should be no unsightly ends or straps left dangling from the loops of the head-stall. They should be so snugly fitted into their places that they cannot work out of their loops.

The forehead band should never be too tight for the horse's comfort, and the small rosettes that lie over his temples should be well oiled underneath and kept soft.

A side-saddle may be made accurately according to all recognized rules, and yet lose nearly all its good effects by being improperly put on; the rider will be made uncomfortable, the horse's back will be injured, and the saddle will eventually have its padding so compressed in the wrong direction that it will be impossible to put it on in the right way.

Every lady rider should know as well how to have her saddle properly adjusted as how to sit her horse or manage the reins. On a well-formed horse, with rather high withers and sloping shoulders, the centre of the saddle should be placed over the middle of the back, and be so arranged that the front part of the saddle-tree shall be a very short distance back of the horse's shoulder-blade, for if allowed to rest upon the shoulder-blade it will interfere[94] very much with the action of the shoulder muscles. It is a common fault of grooms to place the saddle a little sideways, and too far forward on the withers. The well-taught rider can, however, easily decide whether the saddle is in the right position: standing on the off-side of the horse, she must pass her right hand under the arch of the saddle-tree, which should be directly over the withers, and see whether it sits perfectly even, bearing no more to one side than to the other; then stepping behind the horse, but at a safe distance from his heels, she can see whether the long central furrow of the under surface of the saddle-seat from front to rear (chamber) is in a direct line with the animal's backbone, and forms an open space over it. If these conditions are fulfilled, the saddle is properly adjusted. If the horse have rather straight shoulders, together with a plump, round body, the saddle will require to be placed rather farther forward, but with the chamber still in a line with the backbone. On some horses of this shape, the saddle, to be held securely, will need to be set so far forward that the girths will have to pass close to the fore-legs. A horse of this description is not suitable for the side-saddle, but as ladies in the country and in the far West are sometimes obliged to ride such,[95] it is very important for their safety to know how these ill-formed animals should be saddled, because should the saddle be put too far back on such horses, it will be sure to turn.

It not infrequently happens that after the saddle has been placed in the correct position, it becomes slightly displaced while being fastened. To avoid this, it should always be girthed on the off-side, and great care be taken, when fastening the girths, especially the first one, that the saddle be not jerked over to the left; and that in pulling upon the short strap on the off-side, to which the girth is to be buckled, the saddle be not forced to the right.

When girthing the saddle, the lady may place her left hand on the middle of the seat and hold it steady while she arranges the first girth, and with her right hand draws it as tightly as she can, without using violent exertion, or making any sudden jerk; she will then be able, with both hands, to tighten the girth as much as is necessary, doing this with an even, regular pull, so that the saddle will not be moved out of place. Before fastening the other girths, she should step behind the horse and assure herself that the chamber is in a line with the horse's backbone, as before described. If it is not, she must loosen the girth, and, after[96] straightening the saddle, proceed as before. The girth to be first fastened is the one nearest the horse's fore-legs; the second girth is the one back of the first, and should be placed evenly over the first one and fastened equally tight; the third is the leather girth which is intended to keep down the saddle-flaps; this must be placed evenly over the other two, but it is not essential to have it drawn so tight as they, but just enough so to hold the flaps. Most horses have a trick, when they are being girthed, of expanding their sides and abdomen, for the purpose of securing a loose girthing; and girths that seem almost too tight when they are first buckled are often found to be too loose after the rider has mounted. Too tight a girth is injurious to the horse, but too loose a one may cause the saddle to turn. A round, plump horse with low withers will need tighter girthing than a better shaped one. The lady rider should study the shape of her horse, and use her own judgment as to how tight the girths should be drawn, making due allowance for the trick alluded to above. If there is any second person present while the saddle is being arranged, matters may be facilitated if this person will hold the saddle firmly by the off-pommel while the girthing is being done.

[97]

The author has been thus particular in describing the bit and saddle with their proper arrangement, as well as the girthing of the horse, because so few lady riders bestow any attention upon these very important matters; and yet, if one desires to ride safely and well, a knowledge of them is positively necessary. Grooms cannot always be depended upon, and, indeed, seldom know much about the side-saddle; there is an adage which is applicable to many of them: "Too much must not be expected from the head of him who labors only with his hands." In the instructions given by gentlemen writers, useful as they may be in many respects, there is usually a good deal of practical information omitted which a lady rider ought to know, but the necessity of which it is perhaps impossible for a gentleman fully to appreciate or understand; this knowledge the lady will have to gain either from her own experience or from one of her own sex who has studied the subject carefully.

In preparing for horseback riding, nothing should be omitted that can give greater security to the rider, or protect her more completely from accident of any sort. Every article should be of the very best material, so that a breakage[98] or casualty of any kind may be only a remote possibility. The knowledge that everything is right, and firmly and properly placed, creates a confidence which adds greatly to the pleasure of the ride.

[99]

CHAPTER IV.
MOUNTING AND DISMOUNTING.

"'Stand, Bayard, stand!'—the steed obeyed,
With arching neck and bending head,
And glancing eye and quivering ear,
As if he loved *her voice* to hear."

Lady of the Lake.

A novice in riding always experiences in a greater or less degree a sense of trepidation and embarrassment when, for the first time, a horse duly caparisoned for a lady rider is put before her, and she is expected to seat herself in the saddle. If she be a timid person, the apparent difficulty of this feat occasions a dismay which the good-natured champing of the bit and impatient head shakings of the horse do not tend to diminish. If, however, she be accustomed to horses as pets, and understand their ways, she will be much less apprehensive about mounting than the lady who has only observed them at a distance and is entirely ignorant of their nature. The author has known ladies, after their horses had been brought to the door, to send them back to the stable because courage failed them[100] when it became necessary to trust themselves on the back of an animal of which they knew nothing. To overcome this timidity the lady must become better acquainted with her horse, and, to do so, should visit him occasionally in his stable, feed him with choice morsels, and lead him about the yard from time to time. By these means a mutual friendship and confidence will be created, and the lady will gradually gain enough courage to place herself in the saddle.

The first attempt at mounting should be made from a **high horse-block** with some one to hold the head of the horse and keep him still. Turning her right side somewhat toward the horse's left, and slightly raising the skirt of her riding habit, the lady should spring from her left foot towards the saddle, at the same time raising her right leg so that it will pass directly over the second and third pommels. This accomplished, the left foot may be placed in the stirrup.

Another method of mounting from a rather high horse-block, when the pommels are high, is for the lady to face the horse's left side, and, seizing the off-pommel with the right hand and the second one with the left, to spring towards the saddle from her left foot, and seat herself sidewise. She can then turn her body so as to face the horse's head, place her right leg over[101] the second pommel,—adjusting her skirt at the same time,—and slip her left foot into the stirrup and her left knee under the third pommel.

Should the **horse-block be low** and the lady short, she will be obliged to mount somewhat after a man's fashion, thus: Placing her left foot in the stirrup, and grasping the second pommel with her left hand, she should spring from her right foot, and, as she rises, grasp the off-pommel with her right hand; by means of this spring, aided by the pommels and stirrup, she can seat herself sideways in the saddle, turning her body for this purpose just before gaining the seat. In the absence of a horse-block, from which to mount, the assistance of a chair or stool should never be resorted to unless there is some one to hold it firm and steady.

When the rider is obliged to **mount** without assistance and **from the ground**, if the balance-strap, before referred to, be used with her stirrup, she can let this strap down far enough to enable her to put her foot in the stirrup easily, and to use it as a sort of stepping-stone by means of which, and a spring from her right foot, she can reach the saddle sideways. In doing this she must grasp the second pommel firmly with her left hand, in which she also should hold her whip and the reins; on rising[102] she must aid herself by grasping with the right hand the off-pommel as soon as she can reach it. When she is seated, the stirrup can be adjusted from the off-side by means of the balance-strap.

If, however, she uses the old-fashioned stirrup-leather, and there is no assistance of any kind at hand, neither horse-block, chair, nor stool, not even a fence or steep bank from which to mount,—a situation in which a rider might possibly be placed,—then reaching the saddle becomes a very puzzling affair, unless the lady be so active that she can spring from the ground to her saddle. To try the plan of lengthening the stirrup-leather will be dangerous, because, in order to readjust it after mounting, she will have to sit on the back part of the saddle, bend over the horse's left side, and pull up the stirrup-leather in order to shorten and buckle it; while in this position, if the horse should start, she would probably be thrown instantly. Her safest course would be to lead the horse until a place is found where she can mount. If she should have to use a fence for this purpose let her be sure that the posts are firmly fixed in the ground, and that the boards are neither loose nor easily broken.

When mounting, the whip and reins should be held in the left hand, the former with the[103] point down, so that it may not hit the horse, and the latter grasped just tightly enough to feel the horse's mouth without pulling on it. In order to arrange the folds of the riding skirt after mounting, the reins and whip must be transferred to the right hand; then, resting this hand upon the off-pommel, the rider should raise herself free from the saddle by straightening her left knee and standing on the stirrup, also aiding herself by means of the right hand on the pommel. While thus standing she can quickly arrange the skirt with her left hand.

None of the methods of mounting just described—with the exception of the first one—are at all graceful, and they should never be used except in case of absolute necessity. The most graceful way for a lady to reach the saddle, and the one that is taught in the best riding schools, is by the **assistance of a gentleman**. The rider's education will not be complete until she has learned this method of mounting, which, when accomplished easily and gracefully, is delightful to witness. It should be learned after the preliminary lessons at the horse-block have been taken. In using this simple manner of reaching the saddle, the rider will have three distinct points of support, namely, the shoulder of the gentleman who assists her, the united[104] palms of his hands, and her own hold upon the pommel.

Fig. 17.—Lady ready to mount her horse.

The stirrup having been placed across the shield of the saddle in front of the pommels, the lady, holding the reins and the whip with its point down in her right hand,—which must rest upon the second pommel,—should stand with her right side toward the horse's left, about four or five inches from it, her left shoulder being slightly turned back. Then, taking a firm hold upon the second pommel[105] with her right hand, she should with the left lift her riding skirt enough to enable her to place her left foot fairly and squarely into the gentleman's palms, which should be clasped firmly together. This done, she should drop the skirt, place her left hand upon his right shoulder, bend her knee, or give the word "ready," as a signal, and at once spring from her right foot up and a little towards the horse. The gentleman, at the same moment, must raise his hands, and move them toward the horse. The lady must, when rising, press or bear lightly upon his shoulder, and also keep a firm hold upon the second pommel, which she must not relinquish until she is seated. If correctly performed, this manœuvre will place the rider in the saddle sideways. The gentleman should then remove the stirrup from the front of the saddle, while the lady transfers the reins to her left hand, passes her right knee over the second pommel and her left under the third. She will then be ready to have her foot placed in the stirrup. (Fig. 17.)

It will, however, be found very difficult to mount in this manner, gracefully, unless the gentleman who assists thoroughly understands his duties; should he be awkward about helping her, the lady will find it much better to[106] depend upon the horse-block. If, for instance, he should raise his hands too high, or with too much energy, when she makes her spring, he may push her too far over, or even—if she should loosen her grasp of the second pommel,—cause her to fall from the off-side of the horse. This is a dangerous accident, and almost certain to occasion severe injuries. On the other hand, if he does not use energy enough, or neglects to carry his hands toward the body of the horse as the lady rises, she may not reach the saddle at all, and will he apt to fall to the ground on the left side of the horse, especially if she relinquishes her hold on the second pommel. The gentleman must also be careful not to let his foot rest on the lady's skirt, as this will pull her back, and perhaps tear the dress, as she makes her spring.

In assisting a lady to mount, the **gentleman** should first arrange the snaffle-reins evenly and of the proper length, and place them in her right hand, leaving the curb-reins to lie loosely on the neck of the horse. Then, after putting the stirrup out of the way, as described above, he should take a position facing her, with his left shoulder toward the left shoulder of the horse. Clasping his hands together with the palms turned up, he should stoop sufficiently to[107] enable her to put her left foot upon them, and, in raising them as she springs, he must gradually assume the erect posture. When the lady is seated, he should return the stirrup to its proper position and place her foot in it, after first, with his left hand, adjusting her skirt so that it will fall evenly; he should then place the curb-reins in her left hand, with the others. No gentleman is a finished equestrian, nor a desirable companion for a lady on horseback, who does not know how to assist her dexterously and gracefully to mount and dismount.

A lady who is not very nimble in her movements, or who is very heavy, should be extremely careful in mounting not to accept assistance from a gentleman who is not strong enough to support her weight easily and firmly. It will be much better for her to use a horse-block or something of the kind. But if she does accept the aid of a gentleman, the following changes in the methods described above have been recommended: instead of facing her, he should stand close to her side, with his face turned in the same direction as hers: she should then place her left foot in his united hands, and in order to do so must pass her left leg between his right arm and his body. He will thus be enabled to support and lift her with greater[108] ease, and, as she rises, her left leg will readily escape from under his right arm, and she will be able to seat herself sideways in the saddle, as by the former method. During this manœuvre she must sustain herself by the second pommel, as in the preceding instance.

If a horse is restless and uneasy when being mounted, he should be held by a third person, who must stand in front of his head and take a firm hold of the curb-bit on each side, but without touching the reins, which should always be held and managed by the rider only. It is *always* a better plan, when mounting, to have the horse held, although a well-trained horse will stand quietly without such control.

Mounting is a part of the rider's education which should be carefully studied and practiced, for when properly and gracefully accomplished it is the very poetry of motion, and will enable her to display more pliancy and lightness than she can even in the ball-room. There is another branch of the rider's education which also requires careful study, as it is rarely accomplished satisfactorily, and is apt to occasion as much embarrassment and dismay to a beginner as mounting. This is **dismounting**. To alight from a horse easily and well, without disarranging the dress, and without being awkwardly[109] precipitated into the arms of the gentleman who assists, is by no means an easy task, and very few lady riders accomplish it with skill and address.

When assisting his companion from the saddle, the gentleman should stand about a foot from her with his face toward the horse, while she, after taking her foot from the stirrup and disengaging her right leg from the pommel, must turn her body so as to face him. After putting the stirrup over the shield of the saddle, as in mounting, he should then extend his hands so as to support her by the elbows, while she rests a hand upon each of his shoulders. Then, by giving a gentle spring, she will glide lightly to the ground, he meanwhile supporting her with his hands, and, as she descends, bending his body, and moving his right side slightly backward. She can also assist him to lessen the shock as she touches the ground by bending her knees a little, as if courtesying.

Another way of assisting the lady, especially if she be rather stout and not very active, is for the gentleman to clasp her waist with both hands, instead of holding her by the elbows. He should, in this case, stand as far from her as he can while still supporting her, and, as she descends, should make a step backward with his[110] right foot, and turn a little away from the horse, which should be held by a third person, in the manner described before, in mounting.

Fig. 18.—Lady ready to dismount.

Another, and more graceful way of dismounting is the following: The gentleman, standing about a foot from his companion and directly facing her, takes in his left hand her bridle,—as near as he can to the horse's mouth, that he may hold him as firmly and securely as possible,—the lady now drops the reins on the horse's neck, disengages her foot from the stirrup, and[111] her leg from the second pommel, and then seats herself sideways in the saddle, so as to face her assistant, who now places the stirrup on the front of the saddle with his right hand; he then offers his right shoulder to the lady for her support. She, after gathering up in her left hand a few folds of her riding skirt, in order to have her feet free when she alights, places upon his shoulder the hand which holds the skirt, and with the other, in which she holds her whip point downward, grasps the second pommel and springs lightly from the saddle, the gentleman bending over a little as she descends. On reaching the ground, she should, as before described, bend her knees slightly to lessen the shock of the descent. (Fig. 18.)

In all these modes of dismounting, the lady, before attempting to alight, should be sure that her skirt is quite free from the pommels, especially from the second one, and that it is so adjusted that it will not be trodden upon when she reaches the ground, but will fall evenly about her, without being in any way disarranged.

It happens not infrequently that a lady is obliged to dismount without **any one to assist her**, and in this case she should ride up to a horse-block so as to bring the left side of her horse close to it, let the curb reins fall upon his[112] neck, retaining, however, the whip and snaffle-reins in her left hand, and then, removing her foot from the stirrup and her right leg from the pommel, she should seat herself a little sideways upon the saddle. Now, with a slight turn of her shoulders to the right, she should place her left hand—still holding the whip and reins—upon the second pommel, and her right hand upon the off one, and thus alight sideways with her face toward the horse's head. In effecting this manœuvre, she must be careful to retain her hold upon the snaffle-reins and also upon the second pommel until she is safe upon the horse-block; she must also remember the caution given before, in regard to having her skirts free from the pommels.

To **dismount upon the ground**, or upon a very low horse-block, **without** assistance, is a difficult feat to execute gracefully, but some young ladies in the country, who are active and light, accomplish it so easily and quickly that they do not appear awkward. The manner in which this is to be done is nearly the same as that just explained, the only difference being, that the gliding down must be effected quickly and lightly, and the rider, as she passes down, must release her hold upon the off-pommel, but retain that upon the second, also taking care to[113] have the reins quite loose. This mode of alighting is, however, entirely out of place except in the country, where assistance cannot always be had readily, or in cases where the lady is obliged to dismount very quickly.

If the lady rider, after carefully studying these different methods of mounting and dismounting with assistance, will select the one she thinks suits her best, and then practice it a few times with her gentleman escort, she will soon find herself able to perform with ease these apparently difficult feats, and will have no need of resorting to a horse-block, nor to some secluded spot, where she can mount or dismount unobserved. A lady once told the author that the pleasure of her daily ride was at one time almost spoiled by the knowledge that she must mount and dismount in front of a hotel, the piazza of which was always crowded with observers, for, not having been properly taught to execute these manœuvres, she was rather awkward at them. She, however, placed herself under correct tuition, and soon overcame the difficulty. She can now execute these movements with such grace and elegance as to fascinate gentlemen, and excite the envy of rival belles who are still obliged to seek the aid of a horse-block.

[114]

CHAPTER V.
THE SEAT ON HORSEBACK.

"Bounded the fiery steed in air,
The rider sat erect and fair,
Then like a bolt from steel cross-bow
Forth launched, along the plain they go."

Lady of the Lake.

A correct seat is very seldom attained by the self-taught lady rider, for her attitude on the horse is so artificial that she cannot, like the gentleman rider, whose seat is more easy and natural, fall directly into the proper position. Competent instruction alone can enable her to gain the safe and easy posture which will give the least possible fatigue to herself and to her horse. It is true that a natural rider, or she who professes to ride instinctively, may to-day accidentally assume the proper position in the saddle, but, as she has no rule by which to guide herself, and is entirely unacquainted with the "whys and wherefores" of a correct seat, she will to-morrow assume the incorrect position, so natural to a self-taught rider, and the pleasant ride of to-day will be followed by a rough and[115] unpleasant one to-morrow. On the one occasion, the poor horse will receive much praise for his easy motion, and on the next be highly censured for the roughness of his gait, for the lady will not suspect that the real difficulty lies in her own ignorance of a correct attitude, and in her bad management of the poor beast.

Upon the position of the upper part of the body depends not only grace and pliancy, and that harmony between horse and rider which is so highly desirable and, indeed, necessary, but also the ability to manage the reins properly; for, if the rider be not well balanced, her hands will be unsteady, and seldom in the right position for controlling the animal.

But the proper position of the body above the saddle depends upon the correct arrangement of the lower limbs; if they are not in the right position, the rider will lean too far forward, or too far back, or too much to one side or the other. She will also lose all firmness of seat, and, consequently, all safety in riding. This faulty position of the lower limbs has been, and still is, the occasion of much incorrect riding, but is a point which is seldom regarded by the gentleman teacher. He, indeed, cannot possibly know how the legs are arranged, when they are covered by the riding skirt, and probably[116] seldom gives the subject any thought; yet he wonders, after carefully watching and correcting the position of the body, why his pupil does not retain the erect position as directed. A lady teacher of experience is, therefore, much to be preferred to a gentleman, unless the lady pupil is willing to wear, while taking her lessons, trousers similar to those worn during calisthenic exercises.

It sometimes happens that a lady, even after being carefully instructed how to sit in the saddle, and when she seems to understand what is necessary, will yet present a very erect but stiff appearance, as if she were made of cast-iron, or some other unyielding material. This may be due to nervousness, fear, tight-lacing, or affectation. Practice in riding, loose corsets, and less affectation, will soon remedy this stiffness.

Another faulty position is one which may be termed "the dead weight seat," which is only possible when riding on an English saddle. It consists in sitting or bearing chiefly upon the left side of the saddle, the right leg firmly grasping the second pommel, and the left leg squeezed tightly between the stirrup and the third pommel, as if held in a vise. In this position the rider will be fastened to her horse as closely as if she were a package of merchandise[117] strapped upon the back of a pack-horse. She will appear indolent and inanimate, besides riding heavily, and thus distressing and discouraging her horse; for a well-trained horse will always prefer to keep in unison with the movements of his rider, but will find it impossible to do so, when she adopts this constrained, unyielding seat. The rider will also be made miserable, for the constant effort to keep steady by a continuous pressure of the left knee against the third pommel will not only prove wearisome, but will be apt to bruise her knee, as well as strain the muscles of the upper part of the leg, and the next day she will feel very stiff and lame. In addition to which it will be impossible for her to rise in the English trot, or to move her body to the right in the gallop or canter when the horse leads with his left leg. Moreover, should the lady who thus hangs upon the pommel be rather heavy, her horse's back will be sure to receive more or less injury, no matter how well the saddle may be made and padded.

Although the second pommel should be firmly grasped by the right knee, and the left knee be strongly pressed up against the third one, when the horse is unruly or trying to unseat his rider, these supports should not be habitually employed, but kept for critical situations, and even[118] then the body must be kept erect, yet flexible. A rider who depends entirely upon the pommels to enable her to keep her seat is a bad rider, who will soon acquire all kinds of awkward and ridiculous positions, and expose herself to much severe criticism.

The opposite of the "dead-weight seat" is what may be termed the "wabbling seat." This is seen where the old-fashioned saddle is used; the rider, instead of sitting firm and erect, bounds up and down like a rubber ball tossed by an unseen hand. This can be remedied by the substitution of the English saddle, whose third pommel, when used judiciously and aided by a proper balance of the body, will give the required firmness of seat, which should be neither too rigid nor too yielding.

Fig. 19.—Correct Seat for a Lady.
Back View.

The correct seat, universally adopted by finished riders, is the following: The lady should seat herself exactly on the centre of the saddle, with her body erect, and her backbone in a direct line with that of the horse, at a right angle with it. A spectator can readily tell whether the rider is in the centre of the saddle by observing whether the space between the buttons on the hind flaps of her riding-jacket corresponds with the backbone of the horse, and also with the chamber of the saddle. (Fig. 19.) Or the lady can herself decide the question by placing her fingers between these two buttons, and then carrying the former in a straight line directly down to the chamber of the saddle; if these coincide, and if she has placed herself far enough back on the saddle to be able to grasp the second pommel comfortably with her right knee, while the left one is just spanned by the third pommel, then she is in a position to ride with ease to herself and horse, for she now sits upon that part of the animal which is the centre of motion in his forward movement, and in this position can keep in unison with the cadence of his various gaits. Again, her weight being exactly upon the centre of motion, she can with difficulty be unseated or shaken off by the most violent efforts of the horse, for, whether he springs suddenly forward, or sideways, or whirls around, the rider is in a position at once to anticipate his movement, to keep a firm seat, and quickly to gain her balance.

When the horse advances straight forward, the rider—sitting with head erect and her body so placed that its entire front is directed toward the horse's head, or, in other words, that *a straight line drawn from one hip to the other would form a right angle with one drawn along the centre of the horse's head and neck*—must[121]
[122] throw her shoulders somewhat back, so as to expand her chest, taking care, however, to keep the shoulders in line, and not to elevate one more than the other. There should also be, at the back of the waist, a slight inward bend which will throw the front of the waist a little forward. The arms, from the shoulders to the elbows, must hang perpendicularly, and the elbows be held loosely but steadily and in an easy manner, near the rider's sides, and not be allowed to flap up and down with every movement. The hands must be held low and about three or four inches from the body. The bearing of the head, the backward throw of the shoulders, and the curve at the waist, are exactly like those assumed by a finished waltzer, and if the reader is herself a dancer, or will notice the carriage of a good dancer gliding around the ball-room, she can readily understand the attitude required for a correct seat in the saddle.

The right knee should grasp the second pommel firmly, but not hang upon it in order to help the rider keep her seat and balance. The right leg, from the hip to the knee, must be kept as steady as possible, because from a woman's position in the saddle, the movements of her horse tend to throw her toward his left[123] side, and she must guard against this by bearing slightly toward his right. From the knee to the foot, the right leg must be in contact with the fore-flap of the saddle, the heel being inclined backward a little.

The left knee should be placed just below the third pommel, so that this will span it lightly, close enough to assist in preserving a firm seat, yet not so close as to interfere with the action of the leg in the English trot. From the knee to the foot this left leg must be held in a straight line perpendicular to the ground, and the knee be lightly pressed against the side-flap of the saddle. The ball of the foot must be placed evenly in the stirrup, the heel being a little lower than the toes, which should be pointed toward the shoulder of the horse. (Fig. 20.)

Fig. 20.—Correct seat for a lady. Side view.
1, third pommel; 2, second pommel.
View larger image.

If the rider will seat herself in the saddle in the manner just described, she will find that she has a very firm seat, from which she cannot easily be displaced; but in order to appear graceful she must be flexible, and adapt herself readily to the motions of her horse. The shoulders, for example, although thrown back, must not be rigid, and the body, while erect, must be supple; the head be upright and free, and, in the leap, or when circling in the gallop, the body[124] must be pliant, yielding and bending with the movements of the horse, but always resuming afterward the easy erect position. But it must be borne in mind that the above directions in regard to carriage apply to the times when the horse is moving, and need not be observed in full rigor at other times. When, for instance, the horse is standing, the rider may assume a more easy posture, collecting herself and steed simultaneously when she wishes him to move.

[125]

The novice in riding should never be allowed to touch rein or whip until she has acquired a good seat, and a correct balance. During her first lessons, some one should ride by her side and lead her horse, while she, folding her hands in front of her waist, should give all her attention to gaining a correct seat; or, she may practice circling to the right by means of the lunge line, which will prove excellent training, and will teach her to bear toward the off or right side, for it has already been stated that the motion in the side-saddle has a tendency to impel the rider toward the left, and this tendency must always be guarded against by bearing the body a little to the right. Circling to the right, when riding in the track of the riding-school, is also a useful exercise for this purpose, but as riding-schools are not always to be had conveniently, the lunge line will be found very useful, many riders, indeed, considering it even better than riding in the ring, as it keeps the horse well up to his gait.

During a few of the first lessons, that the rider may not fall from the saddle, the stirrup-leather may be somewhat shortened, but as soon as an idea of the proper balance has been acquired and the reins and whip are placed in her hands, the stirrup must be lengthened, as this[126] secures a firmer and more easy seat. This leather will be of the correct length when, by a little pressure on it with her foot, and a simultaneous straightening of her knee, the rider can spring upward about four or five inches from the saddle; but it must never be so long as to render the third pommel nearly, if not quite, useless.

It is better to have the first lessons in riding rather short, so that the pupil may become gradually accustomed to the exercise. As soon as she begins to feel at all fatigued, she should at once dismount, and not try to ride again until the tired feeling is wholly gone. These intervals of fatigue will gradually become less and less frequent, until at last the rider will find herself so strong and vigorous that riding will no longer require any fatiguing effort. In the case of an active, healthy woman, accustomed to exercise of various kinds, these short preliminary lessons may not be necessary; her muscles will be already so well developed that she will not be easily fatigued by exercise of any kind. But for a lady who has always been physically inactive, these short lessons at first are absolutely necessary. The general system of such a person has become enfeebled, her muscles are weak and flabby, and any sudden or long continued[127]exercise would tend to produce very injurious results, so that riding, unless begun very gradually, would probably do her more harm than good.

But after reading all the directions just given about riding, the reader may ask what need there is of so much study and circumspection to enable a woman to mount a horse and ride him, when hundreds of ladies ride every day, and enjoy doing so, without knowing anything about the make of the saddle, or the position they ought to take when seated in it.

Although it seems almost a pity to disturb the serenity and self-complacency of ignorance, we shall be obliged, in justice to those who really wish to understand the principles of good horsewomanship, to point out some of the mistakes of those who think that riding is an accomplishment which can be acquired without instruction and study.

It is not too sweeping an assertion to state that, of one hundred ladies who attempt a display of what they consider their *excellent* horsewomanship in our streets and parks, ninety-five are very imperfect riders; and the five who do ride well have only learned to do so by means of careful study and competent instruction. They have fully appreciated the fact that nature [128] never ushered them into the world finished riders, any more than accomplished grammarians or Latin scholars, and that although one may possess a natural aptitude for an accomplishment, application, study, and practice are positively necessary to enable her to attain any degree of perfection in it. Yet the idea unfortunately prevails very largely in this country that women require very little instruction to become good riders, and the results of this belief are apparent in the ninety-five faulty riders already referred to.

Let us now watch some of the fair Americans whom the first balmy day of spring has tempted out for a horseback ride, and notice the faulty positions in which they have contrived to seat themselves in their saddles. With regard to their beauty, elegance of form, and style of dress, nothing more could be desired; but, alas! the same cannot be said of their manner of riding.

Fig. 21.—Crooked Position in Saddle.
Miss X.

Take Miss X. and Mrs. Y., for examples. These ladies have the reputation of being fine and fearless horsewomen, and certainly do ride with that dash and confidence which long practice in the saddle is sure to give, but we regret to say that we can bestow no further praise upon them. Miss X. has taken a position that is almost universal with American horsewomen, and is exactly the one which a rider nearly always assumes when seated sideways on a horse without a saddle. Instead of sitting squarely, with the entire front of her body facing in the direction toward which the horse is going, she sits crosswise. It will be seen by looking at Fig. 21, that the central vertical line of her back, instead of being directly in the centre of the saddle, is placed toward the right corner of it, and that her shoulders are out of line, the left one being thrown back, and the right one advanced forward. This position makes it impossible for her to keep in unison with her horse when he is moving straight forward at an easy pace. When he changes his gait to a canter the rider will, for a short distance, appear to be more in harmony with him, because he is now turning himself slightly to the left and leading with his right fore-leg, a position which is more in unison with that of his rider. But, after a short time, the horse gets tired of this canter, turns to the right, and leads with his left fore-leg. This change entirely destroys the apparent harmony which had before existed between the two.

The lady, knowing nothing about the position of a horse when galloping or cantering, is [131] [132] ignorant of the fact that he always turns a little to the right or left according to the leg with which he leads, and that she ought to place her body in a corresponding position. She has but one position in the saddle,—the crooked one already described,—and this she maintains immovably through all the changes of her horse's gaits.

Fig. 22.—Crooked Position in Saddle.
Mrs. Y.

Let us now turn to Mrs. Y., who is even a more faulty rider than her companion. She has likewise taken a crosswise position in the saddle; but having given a peculiar twist to her body so that, by turning her right shoulder backward, she can look to the right, she seems to imagine that by these means she has placed herself squarely upon the saddle. (Fig. 22.) As she is riding a racking horse and seated on a two-pommeled saddle, she holds the reins firmly in her left hand and by a steady pull on them she balances herself and keeps her horse up to his gait. But this steady pull will soon ruin the tenderness and sensitiveness of any horse's mouth, and this is the reason why racking horses generally have very hard mouths, many of them requiring to be well held up or supported in their rack by the reins. As this pulling upon the reins also gives considerable support to the rider, many ladies prefer a racking horse. Now notice Mrs. Y., who is attempting to turn her hard-mouthed racker. Instead of doing this by an almost imperceptible movement of the hand, her left hand and arm can be distinctly seen to move, and to fairly pull the animal around. Her right hand—probably acting in sympathy with the left, so tightly clasped over the reins—holds the whip as if it were in a vise intended to crush it. In odd contrast with the rigidly held hands is the body with its utter lack of firmness.

It can be seen at a glance why the lady will only ride an easy racker, for it is well known that on a good racker or pacer the body of a rider in a faulty position is not jolted so much as in other gaits. For this reason also the rack and pace are the favorite gaits of most American horsewomen.

Nearly every lady who rides has an ambition to be considered a finished horsewoman, but this she can never be until she is able to ride properly the trot and gallop, can keep herself in unison with her horse, whether he leads with the left or right fore-leg, and has hands that will "give and take" with the horse's movements and bring him up to his best gait. From this point of view, Miss X. and Mrs. Y., then, are by no means the "splendid riders" that[135] [136] their friends suppose them, but having all the confidence of ignorance they ride fast and boldly and with a certain *abandon* that is pleasing; but by those who understand what good riding is, they must always be regarded as very faulty riders.

Fig. 23.—Incorrect position of legs and feet.
Side view.

Another common fault, against which we have already warned the reader, is that of riding with too short a stirrup-leather, thus pressing the left knee up against the third pommel, carrying the left heel backward and slightly upward, and dropping the toes of the left foot more or less down toward the ground, while those of the right are raised and pointed toward the horse's head. (Fig. 23.) Although the lower limbs are concealed by the skirt, it can easily be told whether they are in the position just described, from the effect produced upon the upper part of the body, which then leans too far forward and too much to the right (Fig. 24); while the rider, in her efforts to balance herself, inclines her shoulders to the left. This is a very awkward as well as a very dangerous attitude, because, by thrusting her leg backwards, the action of spurring is imitated, and, if the horse is very high-spirited, this may cause him to become restive, or even to run away. Should the leg, moreover, as is very apt to be the case, be firmly and steadily pressed against the animal's side, he may suddenly pirouette or turn around to the right, especially if he has been accustomed to carrying gentlemen as well as ladies. This short stirrup-leather and improper use of the third pommel should be carefully avoided.

Fig. 24.—Incorrect Position when Legs and Feet are wrongly placed.

The use of too long a stirrup-leather is apt to be the mistake of those who ride upon the old-fashioned saddle, but is a fault which has become much less common since the English[139] [140] saddle has been more generally used. The objection to too long a stirrup-leather is that, when the foot is pressed upon it, the leg at the same time is straightened, and extends down so far as to cause the rider to sit too much to the left of the saddle. As the pressure and weight are thus thrown wholly upon the left side, the saddle is very likely to turn, and if this faulty position be persisted in, it will be certain to injure the horse's back and may give rise to fistulous withers.

Besides looking very awkward and inelegant, when stooping forward in the saddle and rounding the back without the slightest curve inwardly, the rider will also run great risk, if her horse stumbles or makes any sudden movement, of being unseated, or at least thrown violently against the front of the saddle, as it is almost impossible for her, under such circumstances, to adapt herself to the change in his motion quickly enough to preserve her equilibrium. In all violent movements of the horse, except rearing, the body must be inclined backward, so as to keep the balance. When he is moving briskly in his ordinary gaits, the body must be kept erect; and when he is turning a corner rapidly, it should be inclined backward somewhat, and toward the inner bend of the horse's body; or,[141] in other words, toward the centre of the circle, of which the turn forms a segment.

Here come two ladies who have evidently received very limited instructions in the art of riding. Notice how the head of one is thrust forward, while the other, though holding her head erect allows it to be jerked about with every motion of her horse. It shakes slowly when the animal is walking, but as he quickens his pace to a canter, it rocks with his motion, and, during his fast pace, the poor head moves so rapidly as to make one fear that the neck may become dislocated, while the arms dance about simultaneously with the movements of the head in a way that reminds one of the toy dancing-jacks, pulled by an unseen hand for the amusement of children. The head should, in riding, be kept firm and erect, without stiffness, the chin being drawn in slightly, and not protruding high in the air, because the latter gives one a supercilious look. The head and shoulders should adapt themselves, in their direction, to the movements of the head and fore-legs of the horse, and the arms should be held as steady as possible.

But here come several ladies who have taken lessons at the riding-school and may, therefore, reasonably be expected to be finished riders;[142] but such, alas! is not the case. They have been trying "to walk before they could creep," or, in other words, their lessons in riding have been conducted too hastily. They have begun to try a canter or a rapid gallop before they knew how to sit correctly upon their horses, or even to manage them properly in a walk. This desire to make too rapid progress is more frequently the fault of the pupil than of the riding teacher. Most teachers have an ambition to make finished riders of their pupils, and take much pride in doing so, especially as such a result adds greatly to the prestige of their school. This ambition is often defeated, however, by the impatience of the pupils, who are not satisfied to learn slowly and well, but overrule the teacher's objections and undertake to gallop before they have acquired even the first principles of horsewomanship. Moreover, many of these ladies never take any road lessons, so highly important to all who would become thoroughly accomplished in this art; nor do they remain long enough under instruction in the school, but seem to think that a few short lessons are enough to make them finished riders. They often refuse to learn the English trot, although this is a very important accomplishment for the beginner, as it enables her to gain a correct[143] idea of the balance. Or, if they do attempt to learn it, they insist upon circling only to the right, as this is easier than going the other way.

Again, many pupils will insist upon riding the same favorite horse, instead of leaving the selection to the judgment of the teacher, who is well aware that it is much better for the lady's progress that she should ride a variety of horses with different gaits. He is often driven to his wit's end when two or three ladies who patronize his school, and whom it is an honor to have as pupils, express a desire to ride the same horse on the same occasion. Should he favor one more than the others, the latter will become highly offended, and the poor man in his perplexity is often obliged to resort to some subterfuge to pacify them.

It is not difficult, then, to understand why some ladies, although they have taken lessons at a riding-school, are, nevertheless, not finished riders, their faults being due, not to the instruction but to their own lack of judgment or inattention. It is true that occasionally the teacher, although he may be an excellent instructor for gentlemen, is not so good a one for ladies, or he may become careless, believing that if he gives them well-trained horses to ride very little else is required of him. Or, again,[144] he may think, as many foreigners do, that very few American ladies know how a woman should ride, and are satisfied with being half taught.

It cannot be too strongly impressed upon riding teachers that in every riding-school where ladies are to be taught there should be at least one lady assistant. A gentleman can give all the necessary instructions about the management of the horse and the handling of the reins better than most ladies; but, in giving the idea of a correct seat and the proper disposal of the limbs, the presence of a lady assistant becomes necessary; in these matters she can instruct her own sex much better than a man can.

[145]

CHAPTER VI.
TO HOLD THE REINS, AND MANAGE THE HORSE.

"What a wild thought of triumph, that this girlish hand
Such a steed in the might of his strength may command!
What a glorious creature! Ah! glance at him now,
As I check him awhile on this green hillock's brow;
How he tosses his mane, with a shrill, joyous neigh,
And paws the firm earth in his proud, stately play!"

GRACE GREENWOOD.

The position of the rider in the saddle has a decided influence upon the horse's mouth, rendering his movements regular or irregular, according to the correctness and firmness of the seat; for, if the rider be unsteady or vacillating in the saddle, this will exert an influence upon the hand, rendering it correspondingly unstable, and will thereby cause the horse's movements to be variable. And should she endeavor to remedy this unsteadiness of hand and seat by supporting herself upon the reins, the horse will defend himself against such rigid traction by making counter-traction upon the reins, thrusting his head forward, throwing himself heavily upon his fore-legs, thus forcing the hands of the rider, and compelling her to support [146] the weight of his neck and shoulders. On the contrary, if she be firm in her seat, and not in the least dependent upon the reins, her hand will be light, and the animal will yield a ready obedience and advance in his best pace. The preceding remarks explain why a horse will go lightly with one rider and heavily with another.

A lady should have a thorough knowledge of the management of her horse, and of the means by which she may command him in every degree of speed, and under all circumstances; without this knowledge she can never become a safe and accomplished horsewoman. A gentleman may guide and control his horse, and obtain obedience from a restive one, by a firm, strong hand, and by his courage and determined will; but as a rule, a lady cannot depend upon these methods; she will have to rely entirely upon the thorough training of her horse, a properly arranged bit, her firm, yet delicate touch, and her skill in handling the reins. The well-trained hand of a woman is always energetic enough to obtain the mastery of her horse, without having to resort to feats of strength and acrobatic movements; and a *lady* should never seek to gain prestige by riding restless or vicious horses, in order that she may display her skill in conquering them; [147] though every rider should be thoroughly taught how to control her steed in cases of emergency.

When one sees how little skill most lady riders exhibit in managing the reins, it seems almost miraculous that so few accidents occur to them, and is indeed a positive proof of the excellent temper of their horses. From some mysterious cause, most horses will bear more awkwardness and absurdity in the handling of the reins by a woman than by a man, and will good-naturedly submit to the indifferent riding of the gentle being in the side-saddle, while the same character of riding and treatment from a man would arouse every feeling of defense and rebellion. The probable cause of this difference of action on the part of the horse is, that a lady rider, with all her ignorance of seat and rein, will talk kindly to and pet her steed, and will rarely lose her temper, no matter in what eccentricities he may indulge, and her gentleness causes the animal to remain gentle.

On the contrary, when a man throws his weight upon the reins, jerking and pulling upon them, his horse, seeking to defend himself against such rough measures, arouses the temper of his rider, and this anger is soon communicated [148] to the animal, which then becomes obstinate and rebellious; moreover, a man will often whip and spur for some trivial offense in instances where a woman would simply speak to her horse, or take no notice. Hence, the ignorant horsewoman often rides in safety under circumstances in which the ignorant horseman, who has resorted to violent measures, meets with an accident.

Although a horse may submit to an awkward rider and carry her with safety, still she will have no power to make him move in his best and most regular manner, and there will exist no intelligence or harmony between the two. Yet this same horse, when mounted by a lady who understands the **management of the reins**, will be all animation and happiness. There will soon be established a tacit understanding between the two, and the graceful curvetings and prancings of the steed will manifest his pride and joy in carrying and obeying a gentle woman, who manages the reins with spirit and resolution, and yet does not, with the cruelty of ignorance or indifference, convert them into instruments of torture.

The **reins** should not be employed until a firm, steady position upon the saddle has been acquired, and then, for first lessons, the snaffle [149] only should be used, **a rein in each hand**. It will be better to have the reins marked at equal distances from the bit, either by sewing colored thread across each, or otherwise; this will be useful because, with the novice, the reins will imperceptibly slip through her hands, or one rein will become longer than the other, and the markings will enable her to notice these displacements, and promptly to remedy them. By holding the snaffle-reins separately, in first lessons, the pupil will be aided in assuming a square position upon the saddle, and will likewise be prevented from throwing back her right shoulder, out of line with the left, a common fault with beginners, especially when the reins are held only in the left hand. This rein-hold is very simple; the right rein of the snaffle must be held in the right hand, and the left rein in the left.

Fig. 25.—Snaffle-reins; one in each hand.

The hands being closed, but not too tightly,[150] must be held with their backs toward the horse's head, and each rein, as it ascends from the bit, must be passed between the third and fourth fingers of its appropriate hand, carried across the inner surface of the third, second, and first fingers, and then be drawn over the outside (or side next to the thumb) of the first finger, against which it must be held by firm pressure of the thumb. The thumbs must be held opposite each other and uppermost, the finger-nails toward the body, and the back of the wrists must be rounded a little outwardly, so as to make a slight bend of the closed hand toward the body. The little fingers must be held down and nearly in a horizontal line with the tips of the elbows; and the hands be kept as low as possible, without resting upon the knees, and be about four inches distant from the body, and from four to six inches apart. (Fig. 25.)

This arrangement of hands and reins may be termed the "original position" when a snaffle-rein is held in each hand, of which all the others are variations. In this position,—the reins being held just short enough to feel the horse's mouth,—if the hands be now slightly relaxed by turning the nails and thumbs toward the body, the latter being, at the same[151] time, inclined a little forward, the horse will be enabled to advance freely, and, as soon as he **moves onward**, the original position of the hands must be gently resumed. It is proper to remark here, that when using the snaffle-reins only, the curb-bit should always be in the horse's mouth, its reins being tied and allowed to rest upon his neck, although the pupil must not be allowed to meddle with it. The presence of the curb in the horse's mouth, although not used, has a restraining influence, especially with an animal accustomed to it.

To turn the horse to the right, the right rein must be shortened so as to be felt at the right side of his mouth; to effect this, the little finger of the right hand must, by a turn of the wrist, be moved in toward the body and sufficiently toward the left, with the nails up and the knuckles down, while, in order to aid the horse, the rider will simultaneously turn her face and shoulders slightly to the right. The animal having made the turn, the hand must gently return to the original position, and the body again face to the front.

To turn the horse to the left, the left rein must be shortened, by a turn of the left wrist, carrying the little finger of the left hand toward the body and to the right, nails upward, etc.,[152] while the pupil will slightly turn her face and shoulders to the left. The turn having been effected, the original position must be resumed, the pupil, in all these cases, taking great care that the markings on her reins are even and in the correct position.

To stop the horse, both reins must be shortened evenly; this must be accomplished by a turn of both wrists that will bring the little fingers toward the body with the finger-nails uppermost, the body of the pupil being, at the same time, slightly inclined backward. Now, by bending the wrists to a still greater degree, and bringing the hands in closer to the body, which must be inclined a little forward, and nearly in contact with each other, thus throwing more strength upon the reins, the horse will be compelled **to back**. To make him **move on again**, the hands and body must resume the original position, and the hands must be relaxed, etc., as stated above.

When the pupil becomes more advanced, and can command her horse, in all his gaits, with the reins separate, one in each hand, she will then be prepared for lessons in handling **both reins with the left hand** only, still employing the snaffle, as her touch may not be delicate enough for the curb.

[153]

Fig. 26.—Snaffle-reins; both in the left hand.

For this purpose, the reins being held for the time being in the right hand, the left, having its back toward the horse's head, will seize them as follows: its little finger must be passed directly between the two reins, the left rein being on the outer side of this finger and the right one on its right side, between it and the third finger. This done, the reins must be drawn up nearly even to the marks upon them,[4] so as just to feel the animal's mouth, noticing that these marks are nearly on a line with each other, while that portion of the reins lying within the hand must be carried across its palm to the index finger, to a point between its first and second joints, against which point, being placed evenly with one overlying the other, they are[154] to be firmly held by pressure of the thumb; the right hand may now quit its hold upon the reins. (Fig. 26.)

The reins having been properly placed in the left hand according to the directions just given, this hand, being closed, but not too tightly, must be held at a distance of about three inches from the front part of the waist, with the wrist slightly rounded, the nails toward the body, the back of the hand toward the horse's head, and the little finger down and a little nearer the body than the others. The under surface of the bridle arm and hand, from the tip of the elbow to the first joint of the little finger, should be held nearly in a horizontal line. The elbow must be held somewhat close to the side but not in contact with it, and should be kept steady. Care must be taken, when the reins are held in the left hand, that the right shoulder be not thrown back, nor the left one elevated, faulty positions common to beginners when not otherwise instructed. The right arm should be allowed to hang easily and steadily at the side, the whip being lightly held in it, with its point downward. When the snaffle-reins are held in the left hand as described, we may term this the "original position," of which all the others are variations.

[155]

In order that the horse may **move onward**, the left hand, holding the reins as just described, should be relaxed by turning the thumb downward and toward the body until the back of the hand is up and the finger-nails down; at the same time, the pupil should slightly incline her body forward, being careful not to round the shoulders,—aiding the movement by the voice, or, if necessary, by a gentle tap of the whip. The horse having started onward, the original position must be gently resumed.

In order to **turn the horse to the right**, the left wrist must be turned so as to bring the nails down and the knuckles up,—the thumb being toward the body,—at the same time carrying the little finger slightly to the left, and drawing the reins a little upward. This movement will effect the necessary shortening of the right rein, without allowing any looseness of the left one. The turn having been accomplished, the hand must resume the original position. It must not be forgotten, that while making this turn the face and shoulders must be turned somewhat to the right, or in the direction in which the horse is moving.

To turn to the left, the bridle-hand being in the original position, its wrist must be turned so as to carry the finger-nails up, and the knuckles[156] down, simultaneously moving the little finger toward the right and pressing it against the left rein, both reins being drawn slightly upward. This manœuvre shortens the left rein, without relaxing the right. In this turn the movements of the horse should be aided by the rider's face and shoulders being turned a little to the left. The turn having been made, the original position must be resumed.

The horse **may be stopped** by simply turning the wrist so as to carry the finger-nails up, the knuckles down, and the little finger toward the body, which must be slightly inclined backward. Now, by bracing the muscles of the hand, bending the wrist and carrying the hand farther in toward the waist, at the same time advancing the body, the animal will be made **to back**; though, in backing a horse, it will be better to employ both hands. After having stopped, or backed the horse, to make him **move onward**, a course should be pursued, with both reins in the bridle-hand, similar to that described for the same purpose when a rein is held in each hand.

To change the snaffle-reins from the left to the right hand, as is sometimes necessary in order to adjust the skirt, to relieve the left hand, etc., the following course must be pursued,[157] whether the horse be in rapid or slow motion: While the left hand must retain its position and gentle pressure of the reins upon the horse's mouth, the right must be carried to and over the left hand, its forefinger be passed between the two reins, so that the left rein will be on the left side of this finger, and the right on its right side, between the first and second fingers; both reins must now be carried to the right, across the palm, to the little finger; the hand must then be firmly closed, and the thumb be pressed against the left rein, holding it in contact with the index finger,—the left hand now gives up the reins. In this change, while the right hand is being carried over to the left, this latter must be held stationary, as any movement of it to meet the right hand may cause the animal to turn or swerve from his course, and will at the same time interfere with his gait.

To return the reins to the left hand, the following course must be pursued: While the right hand must remain steady and sustain the gait of the horse, the left must be carried to and over it, insert its little finger between the two reins, so that the left one will be on the left or outer side of this finger, and the right one on its right side, between it and the third finger;[158] then the reins must be drawn through the left hand, and be arranged and held in this hand in the same manner as explained when describing the original position of both snaffle-reins in the bridle-hand.

These various changes must be made quickly and expertly, without altering the degree of pressure or pull upon the horse's mouth. The novice will find it greatly to her advantage to learn the management of the reins before mounting the horse, and can do so by fastening the bit-end of the reins to some stationary object, and then practicing the different changes, until she can perform all these manœuvres without looking at her hands or the reins.

When both the reins are held in the left hand, the rider has not so much command over her horse as when they are held one in each hand. For this reason, unless her steed be exceptionally well-trained and obedient, it will be better, when in a crowded thoroughfare, where quick turns have to be made, to hold a rein in each hand, and this will become absolutely necessary if the animal be hard mouthed or unruly.

When the horse is in motion and the reins are held in the left hand, their **separation**may be quickly effected by carrying the right hand to[159] and over the left, the latter retaining its steadiness all the time, and then passing the first three fingers of the right hand between the two reins, so that they may readily close upon the right rein; the thumb will then keep this rein firm by pressing it against the first joint of the index finger. The position of the hands and reins will then, after a movement of the left little finger to place the rein between it and the third, be the same as described for the original position where a snaffle-rein is held in each hand.

Should the reins become too long when held separately, they can readily **be shortened** by returning the right rein to the bridle-hand, placing it directly over the left rein between the third and little finger, and then, by means of the right hand, drawing the loose rein or reins through the bridle-hand to the proper length, after which the right rein may again be taken in the right hand, as already described.

When the reins are held in one hand, they can be **shortened or lengthened** by simply seizing them at their free, disengaged ends with the right hand, and while this holds them and sustains the horse, the left hand must be slipped along the reins, up or down, as may be required, but without changing their arrangement.

[160]

Another way of holding the reins in the bridle-hand is to pass the right rein to the right of, and underneath, the index finger, and then carry it across the palm, so as to escape beyond the little finger; while the left rein must be passed to the left of the little finger (or between it and the third finger), and then be carried across the palm to escape beyond the index finger. The author cannot recommend this manner of holding the reins to ladies who desire to become accomplished and graceful riders, because the movements of the hands and arms, when turning, or managing the horse, are much more conspicuous; and there is not that delicate correspondence with the animal's mouth that can be obtained by the other methods described.

After the pupil has become expert in riding with the snaffle, she will be ready for the**double bridle**, or the **curb-bit and bridoon**. The double bridle must be **held in the left hand** in the following manner: The *bridoon* or *snaffle-reins* are first to be taken up, evenly, by the right hand and then the second finger of the left hand be passed between these reins (the left rein being between the second and third fingers, and the right rein between the first and second), the back of the hand being directed[161]somewhat upward, with the knuckles toward the horse's head; the reins should then be pulled up by the right hand just enough to feel the horse's mouth, and carried across the palm to the index finger, where they should be held in position by firm pressure with the thumb.

Fig. 27.—Double bridle: all reins in the bridle-hand.
1, upper reins, snaffle; 2, lower reins, curb.

View larger image.

The *curb-reins* are now to be taken evenly by the right hand, and then the little finger of the left hand be passed between the two reins, the left rein being upon the left or outer side of the little finger, and the right rein between the little and third fingers; both curb-reins should next be drawn upward by the right hand until they are nearly the length of the snaffle, and carried across the palm, one rein overlying the other, to the index finger, between its first and second joints, and between the snaffle-reins and the thumb, at which point all the reins must be firmly held by pressure of the thumb against them; the right hand will now remove its hold. (Fig. 27.) The above manœuvring of the reins will give the "original position" for the double bridle in the left hand. All these reins should be of nearly equal length, the snaffle being slightly the shortest, so that, while riding with the latter, the curb may be ready for instant use; this may be brought into play by simply turning the wrist[162] so as to carry the little finger up and toward the waist. And the full power of the curb may be brought into action by turning the wrist so as to carry the knuckles down and the nails up, at the same time drawing the little finger toward the waist.

To shorten or lengthen both the curb and snaffle reins evenly without abandoning the horse to himself for a moment, or without ceasing to keep up his action, the following method may be pursued: The loose, disengaged ends of all the reins that extend beyond the index finger of the left hand must be taken between the thumb and forefinger of the right hand, care being taken during this manœuvre to keep up the support to the horse with this hand; the grasp of the left hand upon the reins must now be sufficiently relaxed to allow this hand to slide along the reins downward to shorten them, or upward to lengthen them; this must be effected without deranging their adjustment; when the proper range has been obtained, remove the right hand.

To shorten the curb and lengthen the[163] **snaffle-reins**: The loose, disengaged ends of all the reins must be held in the same manner as stated in the preceding paragraph, between the thumb and index finger of the right hand, not omitting to keep up a support to the horse; the grasp of the left hand must now be slightly relaxed, and this hand be slid up along all the reins, which movement will lengthen them in the left hand. The grasp of the right hand upon the snaffle-reins must now be relaxed, and the left hand be slid down along the curb-reins, carrying the snaffle-reins with it, until the proper range or distance has been attained, when the right hand may be removed. While these changes are being made, the right hand must sustain the horse by the curb-reins until the left has obtained a firm hold upon all.

To shorten the snaffle and lengthen the curb reins, a course similar to the one just preceding must be pursued, except that in this case the right hand must retain the snaffle-reins, and support the horse by them, while the left hand, in sliding down, will carry those of the curb. In all these changes of the various reins, it must be remembered that after each change has been effected the reins must be held in place by firm pressure of the thumb, as already described.

When **either of the reins** held in the left[164] hand **becomes loose**, it may be tightened, by carrying the right hand to and over the left one, seizing the loose rein by its disengaged end that hangs loosely from the left index finger, and drawing it up as far as is necessary. While this is being done, the left hand must not be removed from its position, and should continue to keep up a steady pressure upon the horse's mouth.

In requiring the horse **to stop**, **to back**, **to turn**, or **to advance**, the management of the double bridle-reins will be exactly the same as stated in the directions given when holding the snaffle-reins in the left hand.

When both **the curb and the snaffle reins** are held in the bridle-hand, they may be**changed to the right hand**, when this is desired, as follows: The right hand must be carried to the left; the second finger of the right hand must be placed between the snaffle-reins (already separated by the second finger of the left hand); and the little finger of the right hand between the curb-reins (already separated by the little finger of the left hand); this done, the thumb and fingers of the right hand must be closed upon the reins, which must, at the same time, be released by the left hand.

To restore these reins to the left hand, the[165] pupil must proceed as follows: Carrying the left hand to the right, the second finger of the left hand must be placed between the snaffle-reins, and the little finger of this hand between the curb-reins; this having been done, the thumb and fingers must be closed upon all the reins, while the right hand releases its hold. These several changes can be made whether the horse be moving slowly or rapidly, care being taken to effect them so quietly that the horse will not be abandoned to himself from want of support, nor interrupted in the rhythm of his gait.

If when riding with the double bridle in the bridle-hand, very quick turns have to be made, or when the horse will not yield readily to the movements of the bridle-hand, it will become necessary to **separate the reins** by taking that of the right snaffle in the right hand; this can be quickly effected by carrying the right hand to and over the left, and seizing the right snaffle-rein with the first three fingers of the right hand; this rein will pass between the third and little fingers and across the palm, so that the loose, disengaged end will escape from between the thumb and forefinger.

Fig. 28.—Double bridle; a snaffle and a curb rein in each hand.
1, 1, snaffle-reins; 2, 2, curb-reins.
View larger image.

In America, most lady riders prefer to guide the horse with the bridle-hand only; in doing[166] this, although they may appear more careless and graceful, they certainly lose much command over the animal. The method at present employed by the best European horsewomen, who *seldom ride with the reins in the left hand alone*, is as follows: The little finger of the right hand is to be passed between the right curb and snaffle reins in such a way that the curb-rein will be on the outer side of this finger, and the snaffle between it and the third finger; both reins must then be carried across the palm, and be firmly held by the thumb against the forefinger. The little finger of the left hand is also to be passed between the left snaffle and curb reins, in a similar manner to that just described, and the reins must be held firm by the thumb and forefinger of this hand. (Fig. 28.) This arrangement may be termed the "original position" for a curb and snaffle rein in each hand.

When the reins are thus separated, the action upon the horse's mouth will be much more powerful than when they are all placed in the bridle-hand. They should be held nearly even,[167] the snaffle being somewhat shorter than the curb, so that the hold or pressure upon the animal's mouth may be made by the former; but should it be required on any occasion to employ the curb, this can be brought into instant use by a slight turn of the wrists, that will carry the little fingers up and toward the rider's waist. To *stop*, to *back*, to *turn*, or to *advance*, the reins must be managed in the same way as when one snaffle-rein alone is held in each hand. In all these various ways of holding the double bridle, the snaffle-reins should, as they pass upward from the bit, always be placed above those of the curb; indeed, it would be rather awkward to hold them otherwise.

As already stated, when the object for which any change of hands and reins has been made is effected, the hands should always resume the original position, as explained for the snaffle-reins when one is held in each hand,—thus, hands four inches from the body, four inches apart, etc. The arms and elbows must be kept as steady as possible, all movements of the reins being made with the wrists and fingers, unless the horse be hard mouthed or badly trained, when the arms will have to be employed and more force will be required. But a horse of this kind should never be ridden by a woman;[168]and the directions herein given will be found amply sufficient to control a well-trained, properly-bitted animal.

The preceding directions relative to holding and managing the reins may appear very tedious and exceedingly complicated. But if the pupil, commencing with the snaffle-reins, one in each hand, will carefully study and practice each method in succession, she will soon find that all these apparently difficult manœuvres are very simple when put into practice, and can be readily learned in half a dozen lessons. When she has once fully mastered them, she will be astonished to find how little management, when it is of the right kind and based upon correct principles, will be required to make her steed move in an easy and pleasant manner.

After the rein-hold has been acquired, and the pupil properly seated in the saddle, she will, if the reins are held steady, observe with each step of the horse as he advances in the canter or gallop, a slight tug or pull upon the reins. This pull will also be simultaneously felt by the horse's mouth, between which and the rider's hand or hands there will be what may be termed a **correspondence**. This correspondence gives a*support* to the horse, provided the rider, while maintaining an equal degree of tension upon the[169] reins, will "**give and take**," or, in other words, will allow the movements of the bridle-hand to concur with those of this tug or pull. A *dead pull* may be made by bracing the muscles of the hand, tightly closing the fingers upon the reins, and holding the hand immovable; but this should never be done, except to convey some imperative command to the horse, or when he attempts to gain the ascendency. This kind of pull will interfere with the natural movements of the horse's head, making him move in a confined, irregular manner, and will oblige him to *force the rider's hand* or*hands;* that is, in order to relieve himself from this restraint, he will give a sudden downward jerk of his head, which may take the reins from her hands, unless she be upon her guard; or else he will move heavily upon his fore-legs, and make his rider support the weight of his head and neck.

Should the curb be used instead of the snaffle, the result may be still worse; because when the curb-reins are pulled upon, the port or arched part of the bit will come in contact with the roof of the animal's mouth, and will press upon it to a degree corresponding to the power used upon the reins, while the curb-chain will be forced against the lower jaw, and if this continual pressure or dead pull be kept up the animal [170] will experience considerable pain. To relieve himself, he will suddenly throw his head either up or down and may even rear. In the latter case, if his rider does not instantly relax her hand, he will be apt to fall backward, which is one of the most serious accidents that can happen when riding. If this rigid pull upon the curb be continued, the horse will be certain, ultimately, to become hard mouthed, if not vicious. This is a reason why so many riders, though having the double bridle-reins, use only the snaffle, and allow the curb-reins to hang quite loosely, being afraid to employ them, as experience has taught them that this rigid hold upon the reins will be instantly resented by the horse. Hence the curb-reins appear to be attached to the head-gear of their horses more as an article of ornament than of utility.

In order that a lady's horse may move lightly and well upon his haunches, the curb will have to be employed occasionally to *collect* and *restrain* him; and when it is managed properly, he will advance in better style than when the snaffle alone is used. The snaffle will answer a better purpose when employed to guide the horse in turning completely around, or in movements to the right or to the left; while the curb will answer during a straightforward [171] motion to keep the animal well up to his action and to bring out his best gait, as well as to collect and restrain him.

An easy "give and take" feeling can be effected by slightly loosening or opening the fingers of the bridle-hand or hands as the horse springs forward; as the hand feels the pull upon the reins, it must yield to this sensation, and will thus allow the animal liberty in his spring or advance movements. Then, as the action of the horse lessens or recedes, the reins will be felt to slacken, when the fingers should be closed, which will tighten the reins, support the animal, and keep him under control. This "give and take" movement should occur alternately and simultaneously with the cadence of each step of the steed, and should be effected without any backward or forward movements of the arm or arms, which must be held steady,—except in a rapid gallop, in which case both the hand and arm will, to a certain extent, have to move to and fro. In the "give and take" movement the reins should not be allowed to slip in the slightest degree, nor to be jerked from the rider's hand by any sudden motion of the horse's head; on the contrary, they should always be held firm between the thumb and the first and second joints of the index finger, the [172] *other fingers alone* performing the alternate action of loosening and tightening the reins.

The reader will be better enabled to understand this explanation if she will take a piece of elastic, pass it around her right hand, which will correspond to the horse's mouth, and then hold the two ends in her left hand, exactly in the manner explained for holding the double bridle-reins in one hand. Now, by making tension on the elastic (or reins) with the left hand, so that the right (or supposed horse's mouth) can just feel this pressure, a *correspondence* will be formed between these two hands (or bridle-hand and supposed horse's mouth) through which the slightest movement of the left hand, or of its second, third, or fourth fingers, will be immediately felt by the right hand; then, while holding the elastic (or reins) firmly, by pressure, between the thumb and index finger, by alternately opening and closing the fingers of the left hand, she will observe that when her fingers are closed there will be quite a tension upon the elastic and consequently upon the right hand, and when they are slightly opened this will become flaccid. The relaxation and contraction of the hand constitutes the "give and take" movement, which causes the horse to move easily, pleasantly, and with perfect freedom, [173] while at the same time he is kept in entire obedience to his rider. Indeed, this movement is *the grand secret of good riding and correct management of the horse, and there can be no good riding without it.*

With this movement there should always be a certain support or pull upon the horse's mouth,—firmer or lighter according to the sensitiveness of his mouth, as some animals are harder mouthed than others, and consequently require a firmer support;—this tension or pressure should be rather light in the walk and canter, firmer in the trot, and very light in the hand gallop. In the rapid gallop, the horse requires considerable support.

In all cases of *restiveness*, except in rearing, raising the bridle-hands will give more command over the horse, as it will cause him to keep up his head, and thus while lessening the power of the animal will at the same time add to that of the rider. On the contrary, should the horse lower his head, and the bridle-hands be held low, the power of the animal will be augmented and he can bid defiance to his rider, unless she can raise his head. She will have to do this in a gentle but firm manner, soliciting, as it were, the desired elevation of his head by raising her hands and quickly relaxing and contracting[174] the fingers, but being careful to keep the reins in place between the thumb and index finger of each hand; she will thus gradually oblige him to raise his neck with his chin drawn in, so that control over his mouth may be regained.

Should he resist this method, the reins must be momentarily slackened, and then a decided jerk or pull be given them in an upward direction; this will cause a sharp twinge in his mouth, and make him raise his head. In these manœuvres the curb-bit should be used, and as the animal raises his head the rider should gently relax the reins, and also be on her guard lest he rear. In some instances a decided "sawing" of his mouth with the snaffle—that is, sharply pulling upon one rein and then upon the other, and in rather quick succession—will cause him to raise his head and neck.

When a horse is obedient, all changes in the degree of pressure upon his mouth should be made gradually, because, if a sudden transition be made from a firm hand to a relaxed one, he will be abruptly deprived of the support upon which he has been depending and may be thrown forward on his shoulders. Again, to pass precipitately from a slack rein to a tight one will give a violent shock to his mouth,[175] cause him to displace his head, and destroy the harmony of his movements. As a means of punishment, some riders jerk suddenly, repeatedly, and violently upon the reins; this "jagging on the reins" is a great mistake, and will be likely to result in more harm to the rider than to the horse, as the latter may suddenly rear, or else have a bad temper aroused that will be difficult to overcome.

When riding on the road there will be times when the horse will require more liberty of the reins, as, for instance, when his head or neck becomes uncomfortable from being kept too long in one position, when he has an attack of cough, when he wants to dislodge a troublesome fly, etc. In giving this liberty when occasion requires, the reins must not be allowed to slip through the hands, but the arms should be gradually advanced, without, however, inclining the body forward.

The movements of the body must correspond with those of the horse and of the rider's hands; thus, when the animal is moving regularly and straight forward, the hands, or bridle-hand, being held firm and steady immediately in front of the waist, the body must then be seated squarely, with its front part to the front, so that the rider can look directly between the[176] ears of her steed. When the animal turns completely around to the right or to the left, the shoulders and head of the rider must also turn a little toward the direction taken by the horse, while the hand must be slightly carried in an opposite direction. When turning a corner, the entire body from the hips upward must incline toward the centre of the circle of which the turn forms an arc, or, in other words, the body must incline toward the direction taken by the horse, and the degree of this inclination must be proportioned to the bend of the horse's body, and to the rapidity of his pace while turning.

When the horse advances, and the hands are relaxed, the body must momentarily lean slightly forward without rounding the shoulders; this will aid the horse in commencing his forward movement. In stopping him, the rider's body must be inclined slightly backward as the hands rein him in. All these movements should be made gradually, and never abruptly.

When a horse stumbles, or plunges from viciousness or high spirits, the rider's body must be inclined backward, as this will enable her to maintain her balance more effectually as well as to throw more weight upon the reins. On[177] the contrary, when he rears the bridle-hand must be instantly advanced or relaxed, the body at the same time being inclined well forward, which will throw the rider's weight upon the animal's shoulders and fore-legs, and cause him to lower his fore-feet to the ground.

A horse is said to be **united** or **collected** when he moves easily in a regular, stylish manner, well on his haunches, with head and neck in proper position, his rider exercising perfect control over him by gentle pressure upon his mouth, and keeping up the regular movements of the animal by a quiet and dexterous "give and take" action of her hands.

He is **disunited** when he moves in an irregular manner, or heavily upon his fore-legs, occasioning the rider to support the weight of his neck and shoulders; also, when the reins are too slack and exercise no pressure upon his mouth, in which case, having no aid or support from his rider's hand, he will move carelessly, or exactly as he pleases.

In *collecting a horse*, the aid of the whip and the left leg will frequently be required, as the rider's hand alone may not be sufficient. In such a case, the left leg must be lightly pressed against his left side and the whip at the same time be pressed against his right[178] side; these in conjunction with the action of the bridle-hand,[5] as heretofore explained, will collect him and bring him up to his bridle with his haunches well under him,—the proper position for starting. As soon as he moves there should be only a light pressure on his mouth. In order to perform the above feat effectively, the whip must not be too limber and must always be held with its lash downward. This simultaneous pressure of the whip and left leg has the same effect in collecting the horse as that of the horseman's right and left legs. Should the horse flag in his movements or move heavily upon his fore-legs, a repetition of this pressure of the leg and whip, in conjunction with the proper movements of the bridle-hand, will bring him well on his haunches and lighten his action.

The horse is always animated by mild taps of the whip, light pressure of the hand upon the curb, a clacking of the tongue, or an urging tone of his mistress's voice. He is soothed and rendered confident by mild and encouraging tones of voice, by the rider's sitting easily, by[179] a gentle hold upon the reins, and by caressing pats upon his neck and shoulders.

In the directions given in this chapter, necessarily involving more or less repetition, the author has endeavored to be as clear, comprehensible, and simple as possible. And the rider will find it of much greater advantage to have these instructions printed, than to be required to learn them orally, as she can read and re-read them at pleasure and have them thoroughly committed to memory before mounting her horse. And, although it has required many pages to present these instructions to the reader, she will find that their application will prove very simple, and will also be agreeably surprised to observe the great control she will have over the feelings and movements of her steed through their agency. Horses are generally very sagacious, and appear to recognize promptly any timidity, awkwardness, or ignorance on the part of their riders, and, according to their temper or disposition, will take advantage of such recognition, either by advancing carelessly or by manifesting trickiness or viciousness. The best trained horse always requires to be kept under command, but by kind treatment and correct management. The horse, when ridden by a finished horsewoman, knows that although[180] allowed to move with a light rein he is under the control of a masterly hand that will aid him in his efforts to please, but will instantly bring him into submission if he does not yield entire obedience.

[181]

CHAPTER VII.
THE WALK.

"And do you not love at evening's hour,
By the light of the sinking sun,
To wend your way o'er the widening moor,
Where the silvery mists their mystery pour,
While the stars come one by one?
Over the heath by the mountain's side,
Pensive and sweet is the evening's ride."

E. PAXTON HOOD.

In walking, the horse moves nearly simultaneously the two legs that are diagonally opposite to each other, first one pair, and then the other. Thus, the right fore and the left hind leg make one step nearly at the same time, and when these have touched the ground, the left fore and the right hind leg are raised and advanced in a similar manner, and so on in succession. In this manner as one pair of legs moves onward the other pair sustains the weight of the animal; and of the two legs that act together the fore one is raised from as well as placed upon the ground slightly previous to the hind one. This is the reason why a horse which walks well and in a regular manner will nearly[182] or quite cover the foot-marks of his fore-feet with those of his hind ones. If the hind-foot should fall short of covering the track of the fore one, the animal will not be a good walker; if, on the contrary, it should pass somewhat beyond the mark of the fore-foot, it will indicate him to be a fast walker, although he may overreach.

In both the walk and the trot, when the horse is moving regularly, a quick ear can detect four distinct beats or tappings of the feet; when these beats mark equal time and sound exactly alike for each footstep, it may be inferred that the horse is a good walker as well as a good trotter, and that all his legs are sound. But if one beat be lighter than the others, it may be assumed that there is some disease in the foot or leg that produces this beat. Horse-dealers will often endeavor to disguise this defect by adopting means to disable the animal temporarily in his healthy leg, as the treads will then be made more nearly alike, though the slight shade of difference thus effected can be readily detected by a quick, experienced ear. These hoof-beats are best heard when made on a hard road.

A horse that is a good walker will move with a quick step, his hind-legs well under him, his[183] foot-taps marking regular time, and his feet measuring exact distances, while he will lift his feet just high enough to escape obstructions on the road, thrusting each foot well forward, and placing it lightly, though firmly and squarely, upon the ground. He will advance in a straight line, vacillating neither to the right nor left, and should be able to accomplish at least from four to four and a half miles per hour.

The walk of a lady's horse is almost always neglected, and as a good walk is a sure foundation for perfection in all other gaits, a lady should positively insist that her steed be thoroughly trained in this particular; especially if she be large and majestic looking, because the walk will then become her specialty. A stout woman does not ride to the best advantage at a rapid gait, but upon a horse that has the walk in perfection she presents an imposing, queen-like appearance. If her steed, however, be allowed to saunter along in a careless, listless manner, all the charm will be destroyed, and the *tout ensemble* will present by no means a pleasing picture.

The beginner in riding should learn to sit and manage her horse in a walk, and should never attempt to ride a faster gait until she can collect her steed, make him advance, turn him to[184] the right and to the left, and rein him back; this last movement is a very important one, with which few teachers strive to make their pupils thoroughly acquainted. Reining back will not only bring the horse under better command, but, with a lady's horse, a short reining back from time to time will improve his style of motion in his various gaits; besides which, the rider may on some occasion be placed in a situation in which, for her own safety, she will be compelled to move her horse backward.

Fig. 29.—The Walk.

To begin the walk: The pupil, having placed herself in the saddle, must not allow her horse to move until she is quite prepared, her skirt adjusted, and the whip and reins properly arranged in her hands. Then, drawing gently upon the curb and snaffle reins, a little more upon the former than upon the latter, and at the same time gently pressing against the animal's side with her left leg, and against his right side with the whip, as heretofore explained, she will thus *collect her horse*, and start him upon the walk. As soon as he has begun to move forward, the pressure of the leg and whip must cease, and the hand or hands must be held steady on the snaffle, the curb no longer being required, unless the animal flags in his movements. The hold upon the snaffle must be only[187] tense enough to enable the rider to feel the beat of the horse's action as he places each foot upon the ground, and to give him a slight support and keep up an even action. Should this support be too heavy, his step will be shortened, and he will be unable to move freely; should it be insufficient, he will carry his head low, will not raise his feet high enough to escape stumbling, will knock his toes against every inequality of the ground, and both he and his rider will present an indolent and listless aspect. Her attitude should be easy and erect, but she should yield herself slightly to the movements of the horse although without showing any lack of steadiness. (Fig. 29.)

Should the horse be too much animated by the reins and whip at the commencement of the walk, he may enter upon a jog trot, or an amble, in which case he must be checked by gradually reining him in until he has settled into a walk. Should he, on the contrary, not be sufficiently animated, he will not exert himself and will move in an irregular and indolent manner; in this case, he must be made to raise his head by a slight pull upon the curb-reins, as already explained, and be again collected and animated by the aid of the leg and whip.

A short, abrupt **turn in the walk** should[188] never be made, if it can possibly be avoided; it is only in case of emergency that it should be attempted, and even then it is more or less dangerous, because, as the horse moves his legs diagonally in the walk, he may, when abruptly turned, place one leg in the way of the other, be thrown off his balance, and fall. When turning a horse completely around, it should always be done in a deliberate manner. This rule should never be forgotten, especially by a novice.

During her first lessons in the walk, the pupil, in attempting to turn her horse to the right, to the left, or completely around, must move him very slowly, pressing her whip and left leg against his sides, and keeping him well-balanced by proper support upon *both* snaffle-reins. In making a **turn to the right**, with a snaffle-rein in each hand, the left hand must not abandon the horse, but retain a steady pressure upon his mouth, while the tension upon the right rein must be increased by moving the right hand and its little finger up and toward the body, at the same time holding this hand a little lower than the left one. The tension upon the right rein should be nearly double that made upon the left, and should be kept up until the turn has been completed. In the turn to the right,[189] the left leg should make a little stronger pressure than that made by the whip, to prevent the animal from throwing his croup too far to the left; and in making the turn to the left, the whip should press more strongly than the leg, in order to prevent the croup from being carried too far to the right.

In attempting **to turn** completely around **to the left**, the same manœuvring, though in an opposite direction, will be required; the above directions for the two hands being simply reversed.

Should the horse fail to turn in a regular manner, or refuse to obey the reins readily, he must be collected, and brought up to the bridle in the manner already described. This will cause him to raise his head and place himself in a position to move in the required manner, and when this is done the rider must slacken the tension upon the curb, and turn him with the snaffle-rein.

In making these turns, care must be taken to have ample space, and it must not be forgotten, that while increasing the tension upon the rein required to direct the turn, the other should not be slackened or abandoned, but should continue to give support to the horse, though in a less degree; and also that this tension upon the[190] reins is much more important when making a partial or complete turn, than when the animal is moving forward in a straight line. For, if the reins be slackened, and the horse left to himself, he will turn in an awkward manner, may get one leg in the way of the other, and perhaps stumble or fall, especially if the ground be slippery, or rough and uneven.

It is a habit with many lady riders, as well as with multitudes of horsemen, to make the turn by carrying the bridle-hand in the direction of the turn, thus pressing the outward rein, or the one opposite to the direction of the turn, against the horse's neck,—the inward rein being completely slackened. This is a very dangerous fault and one that instantly betrays ignorance of correct horsemanship, because the animal is thus left without any support at a time when it is most needed. If a rider has any regard for her own safety, she will remember this very important rule, namely, *to support the horse on both reins when making a turn.*

When all the reins are held in the bridle-hand and a turn is to be made to the left, the fault is sometimes committed of carrying the right hand over to assist the left by pulling upon the left rein; this is frequently done by ladies who have not been properly instructed, and gives[191] them an awkward appearance. When riding with the double bridle in the bridle-hand, if the movements of the horse be controlled by this hand and wrist, as explained in the preceding chapter, the turn to the right or to the left can be effected without abandoning the horse by relaxing one of the reins, and also without the assistance of the other hand. These manœuvres, accomplished easily and gracefully, indicate the well-instructed and correct bridle-hand, the well-trained horse, and the accomplished horsewoman, who will appear to manage her steed more by mental influence than by any perceptible movements of her hands.

To stop in the walk, in a correct and regular manner, is a sure criterion of a good horsewoman, one that has her steed under complete control, for this stop renders him more obedient, and tends to collect him and to bring his haunches into a pliant condition. To accomplish this stop properly, the rider must brace her arms firmly against her sides,—being careful not to let her elbows protrude backward,—throw her shoulders back, hold both reins evenly and firmly, and tighten the tension upon them by turning the hand and little fingers up and carrying them toward the waist, at the same time not omitting to press gently against[192] the horse's sides with the leg and whip. All this should be accomplished by one simultaneous movement, and the degree of tension made on the reins should be in proportion to the sensitiveness of the horse's mouth.

If the left leg and whip be not employed in making the stop, the horse when brought to a stand may throw his weight upon his shoulders and fore-legs,—which he should never be allowed to do, as it will destroy the pleasing effect of the stop, and cause him to become disunited. The animal should be so nicely balanced upon his haunches when he stops, that, with a little more liberty of rein, he can readily move forward in a united and collected manner. The reins must not be abruptly jerked, but be drawn upon, as stated before, in a gradual and equal manner. After the stop is completed, the reins may be so far relaxed as to enable the horse to again advance, should it be required. The stop should always be made when the animal is advancing straight forward, and never, if it can possibly be avoided, when making a turn or going around a corner.

If, when attempting to stop the horse, he should *toss up his head*, the bridle-hand must be kept low and firm, and the right hand be pressed against his neck until his head is lowered,[193] when the rein-hold may be relaxed. In such a case, the rider must be on her guard, as a horse which stops in this manner may rear, when she must immediately yield the reins.

The stop, especially in rapid gaits and when effected suddenly, is very trying to the horse; it should therefore be made only when necessary, and never to display the rider's superior command and excellent horsewomanship; many horses, particularly those having weak loins, have been caused much suffering and have had their dispositions completely ruined by a too frequent and injudicious practice of the stop.

In reining back or **backing in the walk**, the horse bends his haunches and places one of his hind-legs under his body, upon which to rest and balance himself; this enables him to collect force to impel his croup backward. To favor this movement, the horse must be collected, brought to stand square and even on his fore-legs, and then be reined backward by a firm, steady, and equal pull upon both the right and left snaffle-reins.[6] The hands should be held low and directly in front of the body, with the knuckles down, and the little fingers turned up and carried toward the body. During this[194] whole movement care must be taken not to elevate the hands. The body of the rider must bend somewhat forward, with the waist drawn in, but without any rounding of the shoulders, while the leg and the whip must make gentle pressure against the horse's sides, so as to "bring him up to the bridle," and prevent his deviating from the line in which it is desired to back him. The backing must never be made by one continuous pull; but as soon as the movement is commenced, the hands and body of the rider must yield so that the horse may regain his balance, after which he may again be urged backward. These actions should occur alternately, so that with every step backward the rider will yield her hands, and immediately draw them back again, continuing these movements until the horse has backed as far as desired. If, instead of this course, a steady pull be made, the horse may lose his balance and fall, or may be compelled to rear.

When reining the horse back the body must never be inclined backward, as is necessary when stopping the horse; on the contrary, it must always be inclined somewhat forward, as this will enable the hands to manage the reins more effectively, will give the horse more freedom to recede, and, should he rear, will place[195] the rider in the proper balance. Should the rider unfortunately incline her body backward, and the horse rear, she would probably be unseated, and should she pull upon the reins in order to sustain herself and keep her seat, the animal would be drawn backward, and probably fall upon her.

In backing, the pull upon the reins must never be made suddenly, but always gradually, the hand rather soliciting than compelling. When the reins are suddenly pulled upon, the horse is very apt to get his hind-legs too far forward under him, in which case it is impossible for him to move backward.

In reining the horse directly backward, should his croup move out of line to the right, the pressure of the whip must be increased, or gentle taps be given with it upon his right side back of the saddle-flap, the hand at the same time increasing the tension upon the right rein. The taps of the whip must be very light, lest the animal turn too much to the left.

Should the croup swerve to the left, the rider must press her left leg against her horse's side, or give light taps with her left heel upon his side, turning the point of the toe out, moving the leg a little back, and slightly separating the knee from the side of the saddle, in order to[196] give these taps; at the same time she must increase the tension upon the left rein until the horse is brought into line.

When it is desired to rein back, but with an inclination to the right, a slight extra bearing or pull must be made upon the left rein, without relaxing the steady tension upon the right one. A pressure with the whip upon the right side of the horse must at the same time be kept up, in order that he may not carry his croup too far to the right.

In reining back with an inclination to the left, the pull upon the right rein must be slightly increased, still keeping a steady feeling upon the left one; then, by a constant pressure with the left leg upon the horse's side, he will be prevented from carrying his croup too far to the left. Reining back teaches the horse to move lightly, and improves the style of his different gaits, but its effect is very severe upon him, hence its practice should not be too frequent, and always of short duration.

[197]

CHAPTER VIII.

THE TROT, THE AMBLE, THE PACE, THE RACK.

"We ride and ride. High on the hills
The fir-trees stretch into the sky;
The birches, which the deep calm stills,
Quiver again as we speed by."

OWEN INNSLY.

In the trot, the horse moves his legs in the same diagonal manner as in the walk, the only difference being that in the trot they are moved more rapidly. When trotting regularly and evenly, the right fore-foot and the left hind-foot strike the ground nearly simultaneously, and then the left fore-foot and the right hind-foot do the same; and so on alternately, two legs being diagonally upon the ground at about the same moment, while two legs are raised in the air.

The strokes of the hoofs upon the ground are called "beats," and are loud and quick, harmonizing with the animal's rapidity of motion and length of step. The trot is the safest gait for a rider if the horse be free from any defect in his limbs, as he will be less apt to stumble;[198] it is also less tiresome for the animal, because while two legs are diagonally off the ground, the other two support the weight of his body, and thus one pair alternately and quickly relieves the other.

There are three varieties of trot, namely, the jog trot, the flying or racing trot, and the true or even trot. In the *jog trot* each foot is placed nearly in the same track it occupied before it was raised, though somewhat in advance of it, and it remains upon the ground a longer time than when raised in the air, thus rendering the gait almost as slow as the walk. If the horse be young and spirited, he will prefer this gait to that of the walk, and, if permitted, will naturally adopt it. This should be guarded against, and under no circumstances should he be allowed to break into a jog trot; because, however accomplished the rider may be, she will find it a very unpleasant and excessively fatiguing gait, and one which will make her look very awkward. This variety of trot, however, occasions less injury to the horse's feet and legs than any other gait, and, on this account, it is preferred by most farmers.

In the *racing* or *flying trot*, the horse is allowed to step out without the least constraint, the legs being extended as far as possible, and[199] moving straight forward, while the animal spiritedly enters into the occasion and gives out his full power. In this trot all the legs are moved very rapidly, and the hind ones with more force than the fore-legs, in order that the horse's body may, with each bound, be propelled as far forward as possible. Between the two successive bounds all four legs are momentarily off the ground. Very springy fetlocks tend to diminish speed in the flying trot, and hence, not having such elastic fetlocks, a good trotting racer is rough in his action and an undesirable saddle-horse.

In the *true* or *even trot*, the action of the horse is regular, all his limbs moving in an even manner, his feet measuring exact distances, his hoof-beats being in equal time of *one, two, three, four*, and his feet, when moving rapidly, touching the ground only for an instant. There are two ways in which this trot may be ridden: one is to sit closely to the saddle, moving as little as possible, and making no effort to avoid the roughness of the gait. This is the method practiced by the cavalry of this country, as well as by the armies in Europe, and is called the "cavalry" or "French trot."

The other method is to relieve the joltings by rising in the saddle in time with the horse's[200] step. This is called the "English trot," and is the favorite gait of the European and the American civilian horsemen. It is only during the last few years that this trot has been gradually coming into favor with American horsewomen, although the ladies of England, and of nearly all continental Europe, have for a long time ridden this gait as well as the canter and hand gallop, having found that by alternating the latter gaits with the trot they could ride greater distances upon hard roads, and with much less fatigue to themselves and their steeds. The English trot does not wear out the horse so quickly as the gallop and canter; indeed, it has been generally found that the horse's trot improves as he grows older, many horses having become better trotters at their tenth or twelfth year than at an earlier age. The trot in which the hoof-beats are in time of only *one, two*, is very difficult to ride.

In America, many persons condemn the English trot for lady riders, which is hardly to be wondered at when one observes the various awkward and grotesque attitudes that are assumed, even by many gentlemen, when attempting to rise in the saddle. As for the ladies who have undertaken this innovation, their appearance on horseback, from want of [201] proper training or from lack of attention to given rules, has, with but few exceptions, been simply ridiculous. Even with correct teaching and proper application, some ladies, although they acquire the English trot, and do not make caricatures of themselves while employing it, yet do not appear to such advantage as when in the canter or hand gallop. This is also the case with European ladies, who differ very much in their power to make this gait appear graceful. A small, slightly built person, having a short measurement from the hip to the knee, can, when correctly taught, ride this trot with much ease and grace. A tall woman will have to lean too far forward with each rising movement of her steed, as her length of limb will not permit a short rise; she will therefore appear to much less advantage in this gait; while a stout built person will look rather heavy in the rise from the saddle.

However, whether a lady is likely to present an elegant appearance or not when riding the English trot, she must, if she desires to become an accomplished horsewoman, learn to ride this particular gait, as it will enable her to gain a correct seat, to keep a better and more perfect balance, and to become more thorough in the other gaits. From a hygienic point of view, it [202] will prove beneficial, and will preserve both rider and horse from excessive fatigue when traveling long distances. Under certain circumstances, it will also enable a lady to ride a man's horse, which will be very apt to have this trot in perfection, and but little knowledge of, or training in, any other gaits. In the country a regular and sure trotting horse may often be readily obtained, while it will be much more difficult to procure one with a light, easy canter or gallop. This trot, when well cadenced and in perfect time, is very captivating, as the rider escapes all jolting, and feels more as if she were flying through the air than riding upon a horse.

There is, however, one objection to the English trot to which attention should be directed; namely, if the lady ride on a two-pommeled saddle, and the horse happens to shy, or to turn around suddenly, while she is in the act of rising, she is very likely to be unseated or thrown from her horse. With the three-pommeled saddle, however, this accident will be much less liable to occur, but the lady should always be on her guard when riding this trot, especially if her steed be nervous; and to avoid an accident of the kind just named, she should keep her left knee directly under the third pommel, [203] but without pressing up against it enough to interfere with the rising motion, or just so close, that in pressing upon the stirrup and straightening her knee she can rise about four inches from the saddle; the distance between the upper surface of the knee and the under surface of the pommel will then be about one and a half, or two inches. If, in the rise, she does not find herself embarrassed by the third pommel, she may know that the stirrup-leather is of the correct length for this trot. The more rapid and regular the trot, the easier and shorter will be the rise, and the less noticeable the movements of the rider, because, when trotting fast, the rise will be effected with but very little effort on her part, and will be almost entirely due to the rapid action of the horse. To rise when trotting slowly, will be neither easy nor pleasant for the rider, and in this gait she will not appear to much advantage.

In the **French** or **cavalry trot**, the body should be inclined a little backward, being kept as firm as possible but without stiffness, while at the same time the rider should sit as closely to the saddle as she can, with the left knee directly under the third pommel, not using force to press up against it, but simply holding it there to sustain the limb and to assist in keeping [204] it as firm and steady as possible during the roughness of this gait—while the reins should be held a little firmer than for the walk. This trot should never be ridden by ladies after their first lessons in riding, unless the horse moves so easily in it that his rider is not jolted in the least. To trot so softly that no shock will be experienced by the rider as the horse's feet touch the ground will require a thorough-bred of rare formation.

Before the invention of the three-pommeled saddle the French trot was always employed in the best riding-schools, a beginner being required to practice it for a long time, in order to acquire the proper firmness in the saddle; but since the invention of the third pommel the cavalry trot has been almost entirely dispensed with, as this pommel at once gives a firmness of seat that could be obtained on an old-fashioned two-pommeled saddle only after taking many fatiguing lessons in the French trot. It was this fatigue that caused so many persons to condemn horseback riding for ladies, and it also proved a cause of discouragement to the pupils in the riding-school, frequently giving rise to a decided dislike for horseback exercise. But since the employment of the third pommel, it is only necessary for the pupil to take two or three lessons in the French trot, just enough to enable her to understand the movement, after which she may proceed to rise in the English style. However, a knowledge of the cavalry trot will be found useful, as a horse, when reined in from a gallop or canter, will often trot a short distance before stopping; and if the rider understands this trot, she will be able to sit close to the saddle, and not appear awkward by jolting helplessly about.

Fig. 30.—The Trot.

Of all the styles of riding, there is none so difficult to describe or to learn as the**English trot**. We will make an effort, however, to render it comprehensible to the reader. Considerable study and practice will be required to learn it perfectly, but when once learned it will indicate the thoroughly accomplished horsewoman. (Fig. 30.)

To commence the English trot, the rider must collect her horse, as for the walk, and then, as he advances, keep a firm, even tension upon the *snaffle-reins*, because, in this trot, the animal will rely wholly upon his rider to support him and hold him to the pace, without the "give and take" movements of the hands required in the other gaits. It is not meant by this that a dead pull is to be made, but that the support must be firm and steady, with a proper correspondence[207] [208] between the bridle-hand and the horse's mouth. The elbows must be held steady and lightly near the rider's sides, but not close against them. As the horse extends his trot, an unpleasant roughness or jolting will be experienced, which will give an upward impetus to the rider's body; the moment she is conscious of this impetus, she must allow herself to be raised from her horse in regular time with his step or hoof-beats. In this trot, the horse will always have a leading foot, either the right or left, and the foot he leads with is the one to which the rider must rise,—rising when the leading foot is lifted, and touching the saddle when this foot touches the ground. Most riders do this instinctively, as it were, rising and falling with the leading foot.

In *this rise* the action of the horse alone will give the impetus; no effort must be made by the lady, *except* to press slightly, or rather to sustain herself gently upon the stirrup, and keep her knee and instep yielding and flexible with the rise. Care must be taken not to allow the leg to swing forward and backward. The rise should be made as straight upward as possible, the upper part of the body inclining forward no more than is necessary to effect the rise with ease. The back must be kept well[209] curved, and the shoulders square to the front of the horse, without lifting them up, or rounding them in rising.

The **leading foot of the horse** is that fore-foot or leg with which he commences his advance in the gait; it will always be carried somewhat beyond its fellow, while, at the same time, that side of the animal's body which corresponds with the leading foot will be a little more advanced toward this foot, though almost imperceptibly so. Every rider should be taught to know with which foot her horse leads.

When a horse trots evenly and quickly, and with rather a short step, the rise in the saddle will be barely perceptible; but when he trots slowly and with a long step, the rise will have to be higher, in order that the rider may keep time with the slowness and length of his step. In this gait a tall woman will be very apt to prefer a long step to a short one.

In making the rise, the rider must never assist herself by pulling upon the reins, which should be held firm and low to give support *to the horse alone*, not allowing them to slip in the least from between the thumb and forefinger that should hold them steady.

The descent of the body to the saddle must be effected as gently as possible. The right[210]knee should be pressed against the second pommel, and the left foot lean lightly upon the stirrup, the left foot and instep being kept yielding and flexible with the descent, and the body and right leg bearing[7] a little to the right. The descent should be made just in time to catch the next impetus of the horse's movement, so that the saddle will be hardly touched before the rider's body will again be thrown upward to make the rise.

It presents a very comical and inelegant appearance for a rider, whether man or woman, when attempting the rising trot, to elevate and protrude the shoulders, curve the back out so as to round it, lean forward toward the horse's ears, with elbows sticking out from the rider's sides and flopping like the wings of a restless bird, while the body is bobbing up and down like a dancing-jack, out of all time with the movements of the animal. One reason why some persons are so awkward in the rise is that they sit too far back upon the saddle. This obliges them to sustain themselves upon the stirrup obliquely, thus causing them to lean too[211] far forward in order to accomplish the rise more easily. Another cause of awkwardness in the rising trot is an improperly constructed saddle. The seat or platform should be as nearly level as a properly made saddle will permit. When the front part or arch is much higher than the seat, it will be difficult to use the second pommel as a point of support for the right knee, which support is highly essential during the descent, in this trot. It is a common thing to see riders exaggerate the rise by pressing hard upon the stirrup and supporting themselves by the reins, thus rising higher than necessary, and coming down with a heavy thump upon the saddle; to which equestrian gymnastics they give the name of "English trot."

When rising and descending in the English trot, the left leg, from knee to instep, must be held perpendicular and steady; the foot, from toe to heel, must rest horizontally in the stirrup, and in a line with the horse's side. The foot should not be allowed to turn out, nor the leg to swing backward and forward: if the foot be pointed out, this will tend to carry the body and leg too much toward the left, on the rise; and, if the leg be allowed to swing, it will cause the rider to lose the rhythm of the trot. Again,[212] the stirrup must not be too strongly pressed upon, as this will throw all the rider's weight upon the left side, and may cause the saddle to turn. On making the rise, great care must be taken not to advance the left shoulder, nor to turn the body to the left; many riders do these things with the idea that they will enable them to rise with more ease. But this is an error, for such movements will not only occasion fatigue, but will also render the rein-hold unsteady, and the action of the foot and knee uncertain. The body and shoulders must always be square to the front when the horse is trotting straight forward, the body remaining as erect as the action of the horse will allow.

To stop a well-trained horse **in this gait**, it will simply be necessary for the rider to cease rising, sit down to the saddle, and gradually loosen the reins. Many horses, however, are trained to make the stop in the usual way, by having the reins tightened. The advance and the turns are to be conducted in the same manner as that described for the walk.

In the English trot, the horse must be kept well up to his gait; should he appear to move heavily or disunitedly the reins must be gradually shortened, and the animal be collected. Should he step short, in a constrained manner,[213] the reins must be gradually lengthened, to give him more freedom. If he break into a gallop when it is desired that he should trot, he must be gradually reined in to a walk, and then be started again upon a trot, and this course must be repeated until he obeys, stopping him every time he attempts to gallop, and then starting the trot anew. If he trot too rapidly, he must be checked, by bracing the bridle-hand and increasing the pull upon the reins. If the trot be too slow, the hand must relax the reins a little, and the horse be animated by the voice, and by gentle taps with the whip. To regulate the trot, to keep it smooth and harmonious, to rein in the horse gently without rendering him unsteady, and then gradually to yield the hand so that he may move forward again in a regular manner, are very difficult points for beginners to accomplish while still keeping up the proper support upon the bit, and will require study and considerable practice.

A horse should never be urged into a more rapid trot than he can execute in an even, regular manner; if compelled to exceed this, he will break into a rough gallop, or into such an irregular trot as will render it impossible for the rider to time the rise.

An accomplished horsewoman, when trotting[214] her horse, will make no observable effort, and there will be perfect harmony between her steed and herself. When the English trot is ridden in this manner, the person who can condemn it must, indeed, be extremely fastidious. However, it must be acknowledged that it will require the lithe, charming figure of a young lady to exhibit its best points, and to execute it in its most pleasing and graceful style. The very tall, the inactive, or the stout lady may ride this gait with ease to herself and horse, and when properly taught will not render herself awkward or ridiculous, but she can never ride it with the willowy grace of the slender woman of medium size.

Trotting in a circle may be practiced in a riding-school, or upon a level, open space or ground, having a circular track about seventy-five or eighty feet in diameter. It is very excellent practice, especially in teaching the rider to rise in unison with the horse's trot, whether he leads with the right or left leg. For first lessons, the pupil must commence by circling to the right, as this is the easiest to learn, and will teach her to bear toward the right side of the horse. It is very essential that in first lessons she should do this; because in the English trot she will have to guard carefully against inclining[215] to the left in the rise and descent, a fault common to all beginners who are not better instructed.

In circling, the horse will always incline toward the centre of the circle, with which inclination the rider's body must correspond, by leaning in the same direction; if this precaution should be neglected and the horse be trotting rapidly, the rider will lose her balance, and fall off on the side opposite to that of the inclination. The distance she should lean to the right or to the left must be in proportion to the size of the circle that is being passed over, and also to the inward bearing of the horse's body. Should the circle be small and the gait rapid, the inclination of the rider's body will have to be considerable to enable her to maintain her seat and keep in unison with the horse. If the circle be large, say eighty feet in diameter, the inclination will be slight.

In order to *circle to the right*, when holding a curb and a snaffle rein in each hand, the pupil must collect her horse by the aid of curb, leg, and whip, as already explained, and start him forward on the snaffle, holding the right rein a little lower than the left, and drawing it enough to enable her to see plainly the corner of his right eye; the reins must be held steadily,[216] no sudden jerks being given to them, as these will cause the horse to move irregularly and swerve about. Should his croup be turned too much to the right, the pressure of the whip will bring it to the left; if it be turned too much to the left, the pressure of the left leg will bring it to the right.

In *circling to the left*, the horse will incline his body to the left, toward the centre of the circle. It is not very easy to learn to circle to the left, but when once learned, it will be found no more difficult than circling to the right, provided the animal has been properly trained and made supple, so as to lead with either leg. Horses that have been trained to lead with the right leg only will, when required to change and lead with the left, move in a confined, inflexible, and irregular manner, so that it will be impossible to time the rise from the saddle. In riding in the circle to the left, the directions for circling to the right must be reversed, the rider leaning to the *left*, pulling the *left* rein a little tighter, etc. Great care must be taken, however, not to lean too much toward the left in making the rise. The degree of inclination should not in this case be so great as the corresponding inclination when circling to the right, for if it is the rider will throw her weight too[217] much upon the stirrup side, and may cause the saddle to turn.

In practicing riding in a circle, it will be found very advantageous to vary the size of the circle, first riding in a large one, then gradually contracting it, and again enlarging it; or the rider, while practicing upon a large circle, may make a cross-cut toward the centre of this circle, so as to enter upon another one of smaller diameter, and, after riding for a short time in the smaller circle, she may again pass out to resume her ride upon the larger one. These changes from large to narrow circles form excellent practice for pupils, but should always, if possible, be performed under competent instruction.

The first lessons in trotting in a circle should always be of short duration, and the pupil required to ride slowly, the speed being gradually increased as she gains knowledge and confidence. The moment she experiences fatigue she should dismount, and rest, before resuming the lesson.

In the amble the horse's movements very strongly resemble those of the camel, two legs on one side moving together alternately with the two legs of the other side. Thus one side of the animal supports the weight of his body,[218] while the other side moves forward, and so on in alternation. This is an artificial gait, and one to which the horse must usually be trained; though some horses whose ancestors have been forced to travel in this gait, have themselves been known to amble without any training. In the feudal ages it was the favorite pace for a lady's palfrey, but at the present day it is no longer countenanced by good taste.

The pace, however, which is so well liked by many ladies in this country, is a kind of amble, although the steps taken are longer. A good pacer can frequently travel faster than most horses can in the trot. When the steed moves easily and willingly, the pace is very pleasant for short rides, but for long journeys, unless the animal can change his gait to a hand gallop or a canter, it will become very unpleasant and tiresome. Many pacers are almost as rough in their movements as the ordinary trotter; and although they do not jolt the rider up and down upon the saddle, yet they jerk her body in such a manner as successively and alternately to throw one side forward and the other slightly back with each and every step, rendering a ride for any distance very fatiguing.

The rack, at one time so much liked, has become almost obsolete. This is a peculiar gait,[219] not easily described, in which the horse appears to trot with one pair of legs and amble with the other, the gait being so mixed up between an amble and a defective trot as to render it almost a nondescript. When racking, the horse will appear constrained and uncomfortable, and will strongly bear upon the rider's hand; some animals so much so, as completely to weary the bridle-hand and arm in a ride of only an hour or two. This constant bearing of the horse's head upon the reins soon renders him hard mouthed, and, consequently, not easily and promptly managed. The rack soon wears out a horse, besides spoiling him for other gaits, and so injures his feet and legs that a racker will rarely be suitable for the saddle after his eighth year. It is an acquired step, much disliked by the horse, which has always to be forced into it by being urged forward against the restraint of a curb-bit; and he will, whenever an opportunity presents, break into a rough trot or canter, so that the rider has to be constantly on the watch, and compel him to keep in the rack against his will. And although the motion does not jolt much, the aspect of the horse and rider is not as easy and graceful as in the canter and hand gallop, there being an appearance of unwillingness and restraint that is[220] by no means pleasing. The directions for the French trot will answer for both the pace and the rack, except that in the latter the traction upon the reins must be greater.

[221]

CHAPTER IX.
THE CANTER.

"When troubled in spirit, when weary of life,
When I faint 'neath its burdens, and shrink from its strife,
When its fruits, turned to ashes, are mocking my taste,
And its fairest scene seems but a desolate waste,
Then come ye not near me, my sad heart to cheer
With friendship's soft accents or sympathy's tear.
No pity I ask, and no counsel I need,
But bring me, oh, bring me my gallant young steed,
With his high arched neck, and his nostril spread wide,
His eye full of fire, and his step full of pride!
As I spring to his back, as I seize the strong rein,
The strength to my spirit returneth again!
The bonds are all broken that fettered my mind,
And my cares borne away on the wings of the wind;
My pride lifts its head, for a season bowed down,
And the queen in my nature now puts on her crown!"

GRACE GREENWOOD.

In the gallop, the horse always has a leading foot or leg. In *leading with the right fore-foot*, he will raise the left one from the ground, and then the right will immediately follow, but will be advanced somewhat beyond the left one; and this is the reason why, in this case, the right side is called the "leading side." In the descent of the fore-feet, the left one will touch the ground first, making the first beat, and will[222] be immediately followed by the leading or right fore-foot which will make the second beat. The hind-legs are moved in a similar way, the left hind-foot making the third beat, and the right one the fourth. These beats vary in accordance with the adjustment of the horse's weight, but when he gallops true and regular, as in the canter, the hoof-beats distinctly mark *one*, *two*, *three*, *four*. In the rapid gallop the hoof-beats sound in the time of *one-two*, or *one-two-three*.

In *leading with the left foot*, the left side of the horse will be advanced slightly and the left leg be carried somewhat beyond the right, the action being just the reverse of that above described when leading with the right leg. In this case the left side is termed the "leading side." The hoof-beats of horses in the trot and gallop have been admirably rendered by Bellini, in the opera of "Somnambula," just previous to the entrance of Rudolfo upon the stage. There are three kinds of gallop, namely, the *rapid*or *racing*, the *hand gallop*, and the *canter.*

The canter is a slow form of galloping, which the horse performs by throwing his weight chiefly upon his hind-legs, the fore ones being used more as supports than as propellers.[223] Horses will be found to vary in their modes of cantering, so much so as to render it almost impossible to describe them accurately. Small horses and ponies have a way of cantering with a loose rein, and without throwing much weight upon their haunches, moving their feet rapidly, and giving pattering hoof-beats. Most ponies on the Western prairies canter in this manner, and it is said to be a very easy gait for a horseman though very unpleasant, from its joltings, for a lady.

Another canter is what might be termed the "canter of a livery-stable horse." This appears to be partly a run and partly a canter, a peculiarity which is due to the fact that one or more of the animal's feet are unsound, and he adopts this singular movement for the purpose of obtaining relief. The little street gamins in London recognize the sound of this canter at once, and will yell out, in time with the horse's hoof-beats, "three pence, two pence," in sarcastic derision of the lady's hired horse and the unhappy condition of his feet.

In the true canter, which alone is suitable for a lady, the carriage of the horse is grand and elegant. In this gait, the animal has his hind-legs well under his body, all his limbs move regularly, his neck has a graceful curve, and[224] responds to the slightest touch of the rider's hand upon the reins. A horse that moves in this manner is one for display; his grand action will emphasize the grace of a finished rider, and the appearance of the *tout ensemble* will be the extreme of elegance and well-bred ease.

Horses intended for ladies' use are generally trained to lead in the canter with the right or off fore-foot. Most lady riders, whose lessons in riding have been limited, sit crosswise upon their saddles. This position, without their being aware of it, places them more in unison with the horse's movements, and thereby renders the canter with this lead the easiest gait for them. But if a horse be constantly required to canter with this lead he will soon become unsound in his left hind-leg, because in leading with the right fore-foot he throws the greater part of his weight upon his left hind-leg, and thus makes it perform double duty. For this reason the majority of ladies' horses, when the canter is their principal gait, will be found to suffer from strained muscles, tendons, and articulations.

A finished rider will from time to time relieve her horse by changing the lead to the left leg, or else she will change the canter to a trot. Should her horse decidedly refuse to lead with the foot required, whether right or left, it may be inferred that he is unsound in that leg or foot; in which case he should be favored, and permitted to make his own lead, while the canter should frequently be changed to a walk.

Fig. 31.—Entering upon the Canter with the Right Leg leading.

To **commence the canter**, the horse must be brought to a walk, or to a stand, then be placed on his haunches, and collected by means of the curb, left leg, and whip; and then the bridle-hand must be raised, while the second, third, and fourth fingers are moved to and fro, so as to give gentle pulls upon the curb-reins, thus soliciting the animal to raise his fore-feet. In performing these manœuvres, the rider must be careful to direct the leg with which she desires her horse to lead. This may be done as follows: If she desires to have the **right leg lead**, the tension upon the left curb-rein must, *just before* the animal rises to take his first step, be increased enough to make him incline his head so far to the left that the rider can see his left nostril, while, simultaneously, her left leg must press against his side. By these means, the horse will be prompted to place himself obliquely, with his head rather to the left, and his croup to the right.

The rider, if seated exactly in the centre of her saddle, must take a position corresponding[227]
[228] to that of the horse, by throwing her right hip and shoulder somewhat forward, her face looking toward the animal's head, while her body is held erect with the shoulders gracefully inclined backward, and the hollow of the back well curved inward. Any stiffness or rigidity of the body must

be guarded against in these movements and positions. The rider must hold herself in a pliant manner, and yield to the motions of the horse. The left leg must be held steady, the knee being placed directly underneath the third pommel, and care must be taken not to press upon the stirrup, as this will tend to raise the body from the saddle, and convey its weight almost wholly to the left side.

The hands must be held somewhat elevated and steady, and, as the horse advances, the tension on the reins must be even, so that the fingers can feel every cadence of his step, and give and take with his movements. Unlike the trot, in which the horse must be supported by the snaffle, the canter will require the curb to sustain and keep up his action. After the animal has started in the canter with the right leg leading, should he incline too much to the left, the tension upon the right rein must be increased, so as to turn his head more to the right and bring him to the proper inclination[229] for the lead of the right leg. This correction must be effected gradually and lightly, so as not to disturb the gait, or cause him to change his leading leg. This canter with the right leg leading is very easy to learn, and will not require much practice to master.

However, should the horse fail to obey these indications of the left rein and leg, and start off in a false and disunited manner, as explained under "the turn in the canter," another course should be pursued, namely: the tension upon the right or off curb-rein must be increased so as to bring the animal's nose to the right, as if he were going to turn to the right on a curve, while at the same time the left leg must be pressed against his side in order to have him carry his croup slightly to the right. Now he must be made to lift his fore-feet by increased tension on both curb reins, and then be urged forward. As he advances, the hands should be extended a little to give him more freedom in the spring forward, and he will then naturally lead with the right side advanced. When once started in this gait, the rider must equalize the tension upon the reins, having placed herself in the saddle, in the manner explained for the canter. To have him lead with the left leg, a similar but reversed course must be pursued, using[230]pressure with the whip, instead of the leg, to make him place his croup to the left.

To canter with the **left leg leading** will be found more difficult to acquire, and will demand more study and practice. The horse, having been collected, must then be inclined obliquely to the right. To accomplish this, the rider must increase the tension of the right curb-rein, and press her whip against the animal's right side, which will urge his head to the right and his croup to the left. In order that the position of the rider's body may correspond with that of the horse, her left hip and shoulder must be slightly advanced, in precedence of her right hip and shoulder. It will be observed that the manœuvring in this lead is similar to that in which the right leg leads, except that the *direction* of the positions, of the management of the reins, and of the horse's bearing during the canter is simply reversed; in either lead, however, the tension or bearing upon the reins, as the horse advances in the canter, must be equal.

It may be proper to state here that, as the amount of tension needed upon the reins when cantering varies considerably with different horses, some needing only the lightest touch, the rider will, consequently, have to ascertain for herself how much will be suitable for her[231] horse. Some horses, after having fairly started in the canter, will bend their necks so as to carry their chin closer to the throat, while others again will extend the neck so as to carry the chin forward. In the first instance, the reins will have to be shortened in order to give the animal the proper support in the gait, as well as to keep up the correspondence between his mouth and the bridle-hand; in the latter they will require to be lengthened, to give him more freedom in his movement. Should the reins be held too short, or the rider's hand be heavy and unyielding, the horse will be confined in his canter; should the reins be held too long, he will canter carelessly, and will either move heavily upon his fore-legs, or break into an irregular trot.

A rider may by attending to the following directions readily determine whether her horse be leading with the leg she desires, and also whether he be advancing in a true and united manner: If he be moving regularly and easily, with a light play upon the reins in harmony with the give and take movements of the hand, his head being slightly inclined in a direction opposite to that of the leading leg, and his action being smooth and pleasant to the rider, he will, as a rule, be cantering correctly. But if[232] he be moving roughly and unevenly, giving the rider a sensation of jolting, if his head is inclined toward the same side as that of the leading leg, and he does not yield prompt obedience to the reins, then he is not cantering properly, and should be immediately stopped, again collected, and started anew. If necessary this course should be repeated until he advances regularly and unitedly.

Some horses, after having fairly entered upon the canter, will change the leading leg, and will even keep changing from one to the other, at short intervals. This is a bad habit, and one that will never be attempted by a well-trained animal, unless his rider does not understand how to support him correctly and to keep him leading with the required leg. A horse should never be allowed to change his leading leg except at the will of his rider; and should he do so, he should be chidden and stopped instantly, and then started anew.

If the rider when trotting rapidly wishes to change to a canter, she must first moderate the trot to a walk, because the horse will otherwise be apt to break from the trot into a rapid gallop. Should he insist upon trotting, when it is desired that he should canter, he must be stopped, collected with the curb-bit, as heretofore[233] described in the directions for commencing the canter, and started anew. This course must be repeated every time he disobeys, and be continued until he is made to canter.

It may be remarked here that, in the canter, whenever the horse moves irregularly, advances heavily upon his fore-legs, thus endeavoring to force his rider's hand, or when he fails to yield ready obedience, he should always be stopped, collected, and started anew,—repeating this course, if necessary, several times in succession. Should the animal, however, persist in his disobedience, pull upon the reins, and get his head down, his rider must, as he moves on, gently yield the bridle-reins, and each time he pulls upon them she must gradually, but firmly, increase the tension upon them, by drawing them in toward her waist. This counter-traction must be continued until the horse yields to the bridle and canters properly. When he pulls upon the reins his rider in advancing her hands to yield the reins should be careful to keep her body erect, and not allow it to be pulled forward.

The turn in the canter. In turning to *the right*, if the horse is leading with the inward leg, or the one toward the centre of the circle of which the distance to be turned forms an[234] arc, in the present instance the right fore-leg which is followed by the right hind-leg, he is said to be true and united, and will be able to make the turn safely. Should the turn be made toward *the left*, the horse leading with his inward or left fore-leg, followed by the left hind-leg, he will likewise be true and united.

On the contrary, the animal will be disunited when, in cantering to the right, he leads with the right fore-leg followed by the left hind-leg, or when he leads with the left fore-leg followed by the right hind-leg. In either case, from want of equilibrium in action and motion, a very slight obstruction may make him fall.

In turning toward the left, in a canter, the horse will be disunited if he leads with the left fore-leg followed by the right hind-leg, or if he leads with the right fore-leg followed by the left hind-leg, as in the preceding instance, he will be liable to fall. A horse is said to go false when, in turning to the right, in the canter, he leads with both left legs, or advances his left side beyond his right; also, when in cantering to the left he leads with both right legs or advances his right side beyond his left; in either of these false movements he will be very liable to fall.

When it is desired to **turn to the right**, in[235] the canter, the horse must be kept well up to the bridle, so as to place his haunches forward and well under him, thus keeping him light on his fore-legs, and preventing his bearing too heavily upon his shoulders; and, while the inward rein is being tightened in order to make the turn, the outward one must continue to support the horse, being just loose enough to allow him to incline his head and neck toward the inner side of the turn. Pressure from the left leg of the rider will keep the animal from inclining his haunches too much to the left, during the turn. Should the steed be turned merely by means of the inward rein, without being kept well up to the bridle, and without either leg or whip being used upon his outer side, he will turn heavily upon his forehand, and will be obliged to change to the outward leg in order to support himself. This will cause him, after the turn has been accomplished, to advance in a disunited way in the canter.

When it is desired to **turn to the left**, the instructions in the preceding paragraph may be pursued, the directions, however, being reversed and pressure with the whip being employed instead of that with the leg.

Sudden, sharp turns, are always dangerous, however sure-footed the horse may be, and especial[236] care should be taken not to turn quickly to the right when the left fore-leg leads, nor to the left when the right fore-leg leads, as in either case the animal will almost certainly be thrown off his balance. In turning a "sharp corner," especially when the rider cannot see what she is liable to encounter, it will be better for her to make the turn at a walk, and keep her own side of the road, the right.

The stop in the canter. In bringing the horse to a stand, in the canter, he should be well placed on his haunches by gradually increasing the pull upon the curb-reins just as his fore-feet are descending toward the ground; the hind-feet being then well under the horse will complete the stop. The rider must guard against leaning forward, as this will not only prevent the horse from executing the stop in proper form, but should he suddenly come to a stand, it will throw her still farther forward, and the reins will become relaxed. Now, while she is thus leaning forward, should the animal suddenly raise his head, the two heads will be very likely to come into unpleasant contact; or should the horse stumble, his liability to fall will be increased, because the rider will not be in a proper position to support him, and will increase the weight upon his shoulders, by being so far forward.

[237]

Many ladies not only lean forward while effecting the stop, but also draw the bridle-hand to the left, and carry the bridle-arm back so that the elbow projects behind and beyond the body, while at the same time they elevate the shoulder on this side. This is an extremely awkward manner of bringing a horse to a stand. The stop should be made in the same manner as that described in the walk, that is, by gradually drawing the bridle-hand toward the waist, etc.

Nearly all horses, unless exceptionally well trained, will trot a short distance before coming to a stand in the canter or gallop, and it is here that a knowledge of the French or cavalry trot will prove essential, because the rider will then comprehend the motion, and will sit closely to the saddle until the horse stops. In all cases, the horse should be brought to a stand in a regular, collected manner, so that with a little more liberty of rein he can promptly reënter upon the canter, should this be desired.

[238]

CHAPTER X.
THE HAND GALLOP.—THE FLYING GALLOP.

"Now we're off like the winds to the plains whence they came;
And the rapture of motion is thrilling my frame!
On, on speeds my courser, scarce printing the sod,
Scarce crushing a daisy to mark where he trod!
On, on like a deer, when the hound's early bay
Awakes the wild echoes, away, and away!
Still faster, still farther, he leaps at my cheer,
Till the rush of the startled air whirs in my ear!
Now 'long a clear rivulet lieth his track,—
See his glancing hoofs tossing the white pebbles back!
Now a glen dark as midnight—what matter?—we'll down
Though shadows are round us, and rocks o'er us frown;
The thick branches shake as we're hurrying through,
And deck us with spangles of silvery dew!"

GRACE GREENWOOD.

The hand gallop is an intermediate gait between the canter and the flying gallop. Its motion, though rather rapid, is smooth, easy, and very agreeable for both rider and steed. Nearly all horses, especially spirited ones, prefer this movement to any other; the bronchos on the plains of the far West will keep up this long, easy lope or hand gallop for miles, without changing their gait, or requiring their riders to draw rein, and without any apparent fatigue. This pace is likewise a favorite one with riding[239]parties, as the motion is so smooth that conversation can be kept up without difficulty. If the animal's movements are light, supple, and elegant, the lady rider presents a very graceful appearance when riding this gait, as the reactions in it are very mild; it is the gait *par excellence*, for a country ride.

On a breezy summer morning, there is nothing more exhilarating than a ride at a hand gallop, on a willing, spirited horse; it brightens the spirits, braces the nerves, refreshes the brain, and enables one to realize that "life is worth living."

"I tell thee, O stranger, that unto me
The plunge of a fiery steed
Is a noble thought,—to the brave and free
It is music, and breath, and majesty,—
'Tis the life of a noble deed;
And the heart and the mind are in spirit allied
In the charm of a morning's glorious ride."

Let all gloomy, dyspeptic invalids try the cheering effects of a hand gallop, that they may catch a glimpse of the sunlight that is always behind even the darkest cloud of despondency.

When the horse is advancing in a collected canter, if the rider will animate him a little more by gentle taps with the whip, and then as he springs forward give him more liberty of the curb-rein, he will enter upon a **hand gallop**. In this gait he will lead either with the[240] left or the right foot, but the oblique position of his body will be very slight. The management of the reins, the turns to the right or to the left, the stop, and the position of the rider's body, must, in this gait be the same as in the canter, except that the body need not be quite so erect, and the touch upon the reins must be very light, barely appreciable.

If riding a spirited horse, the lady must be upon her guard, lest he increase his speed and enter into a flying or racing gallop. Any horse is liable to do this when he has not been properly exercised, especially if he is with other horses, when a spirit of rivalry is aroused, and he sometimes becomes almost unmanageable from excitement. Many livery-stable horses, although quiet enough in the city, will, when ridden upon country roads, especially in the spring, require all the skill of their riders to keep them under control. The change from the stone and brick of the city or town to the odor of the fresh grass and the sight of green fields has an exhilarating effect upon them, and makes them almost delirious with gladness, so that they act like anything but sensible, quiet, well-worked horses.

When her horse manifests any such disposition, the rider must retain her presence of[241]mind, and not permit any nervousness or excitement on her part to increase that of her horse. She must keep him well under the control of the curb-bit, and not allow him to increase his speed; when he endeavors to do so, she must sit erect, and every time his fore-feet touch the ground she must tighten the curb-reins, by drawing them gradually but firmly toward her waist. She will thus check the animal's desire to increase his speed, by compelling him to rest upon her hand at short intervals until he can be brought under command and again made obedient. Care must be taken not to make this strong pull upon the animal's mouth constant, as this will be more apt to increase than to lessen his speed, and will also prevent her from turning him readily should she encounter any object upon the road.

Should the horse, however, continue to disobey the commands of his rider, and persist in his efforts to increase his speed, she must then lean well back, and "saw his mouth" with the snaffle-reins, that is, she must pull first one of these reins and then the other in rapid succession; this may cause him to swerve out of a straight course, but if he has a snaffle-bit separate from the curb this sawing will generally have the desired effect, and stop him.

[242]

If the horse should get his head down and manifest a disposition to change the full gallop into a runaway, the rider must, as she values her own safety, keep her body well inclined backward, for some horses, when excited, will, while their riders are endeavoring to check or control them, kick up as they gallop along, and the rider, unless she is prepared for such movements, will be in danger of being thrown. In such a case every effort must be made to raise the horse's head. To do this, the rider must slacken the curb-reins for a moment, and then suddenly give them a strong, decided jerk upward; this will cause a severe shock to the horse's mouth, and make him raise his head and stop suddenly, a movement that may throw her toward or upon the front of the saddle with considerable force, unless she guard herself against such an accident by leaning well back.

Should the horse, when galloping at full speed, turn a corner in spite of the efforts of his rider, she must keep a steady pull upon the outer curb-rein, and lean well back and in toward the centre of the curve which the horse is describing in his turn. All this must be done quickly, or she will lose her balance and fall off upon the outer side.

During all these violent efforts of the horse the rider must keep a firm, steady seat, pressing her left knee up strongly against the third pommel, and at the same time holding the second clasped firmly by the bend of her right knee. If she recollects to do all this, there will be little cause for alarm, as it will then be very difficult for her horse to unseat her. The combined balance and grip of limbs will give her a firmer seat than it is possible for a man to acquire in his saddle.

Fig. 32.—The Flying Gallop.

In the flying or racing gallop the horse manifests the utmost capabilities of his speed, his body at every push of his hind-legs being raised from the ground so quickly that he will appear as if almost flying through the air; hence the name "flying gallop." In this gait it is unimportant with which leg the horse leads, provided the advance of the hind-leg on the same side as that of the leading one be made correspondingly. It is advisable that every lady rider should learn to sit the flying gallop, as she will then be better able to maintain her seat, and to manage her horse should she ever have the misfortune to be run away with. (Fig. 32.)

Many ladies, when riding in the country, enjoy a short exhilarating flying gallop; and for their benefit a few instructions are here given[245] [246] that will enable them to indulge their *penchant* for rapid riding, without danger to themselves, or injury to their horses. Before the lady attempts rapid riding, however, she must be thoroughly trained in all the other gaits of the animal, must possess strong, healthy nerves, and must have sufficient muscular power in her arms to hold and manage her horse, and to stop him whenever occasion requires; she must also have fitted to his mouth a curb-bit which possesses sufficient power to control him and to bring him to a stand, when this is desired. Above all, her horse must be sure-footed, and free from any and every defect that might occasion stumbling.

Every point having been carefully attended to, and the lady being ready for the ride, she must sit firmly upon the centre of the saddle, grasping the second and third pommels, as described above. She must be careful not to press strongly upon the stirrup, as this will tend to raise her body from the saddle. From the hips down the body and limbs must be held as immovable as possible. The body, below the waist, must by its own weight, aided by the clasp of the right and left legs upon their respective pommels, secure a firm seat upon the saddle. From the waist up the body must be[247] pliable, the shoulders being well back, and the back curved in, so that the rider may keep her balance, and control the horse's action. The reins must be held separately, in the manner described for holding the double bridle-reins in both hands. The animal must be ridden and supported by the snaffle-reins, the curb being held ready to check him instantly should he endeavor to obtain the mastery. The hands must be held low, and about six or eight inches apart, and the rider's body must lean back somewhat.

Leaning forward is a favorite trick of the horse-jockey when riding a race, as it is supposed to assist the horse, and also enable the rider to raise himself on the stirrups; but as lady riders are not horse-jockeys, and are not supposed to ride for a wager, but simply for the enjoyment of an exhilarating exercise, it will not be at all necessary for them to assume this stooping posture. Many of the best horsemen, when riding at full gallop in the hunting field, or on the road, prefer to incline the body somewhat backward, this having been found the safest as well as most graceful position for the rider.

As the horse moves rapidly forward, the rider, while keeping a firm hand upon the snaffle-reins[248] so as to give full support to the horse, must be sure with every stride of the animal to "give and take," and this motion, instead of being limited to the hands and wrists, as in all other gaits, must in this one embrace the whole of the fore-arms, which, using the elbows as a hinge, should move as far as is necessary.

To **stop the horse** in a flying gallop, the curb-reins must be drawn upward and toward the waist gradually, for should they be pulled upon suddenly it would be apt to stop him so abruptly that he would either become overbalanced, or cross his legs, and fall.

In this gait, the rider should never attempt to turn her horse except upon a very large circle, because, even when in the proper position, unless she possesses great muscular power, she will be almost certain to be thrown off on the outward side by the forcible and vigorous impetus imparted.

[249]

CHAPTER XI.

THE LEAP.—THE STANDING LEAP.—THE FLYING LEAP.

"Soft thy skin as silken skein,
Soft as woman's hair thy mane,
Tender are thine eyes and true;
All thy hoofs like ivory shine,
Polished bright; oh, life of mine,
Leap, and rescue Kurroglou!"
Kyrat, then, the strong and fleet,
Drew together his four white feet,
Paused a moment on the verge,
Measured with his eye the space,
And into the air's embrace
Leaped as leaps the ocean serge.

LONGFELLOW,
The Leap of Roushan Beg.

A lady rider who has the nerve and confidence to ride a hand gallop, or a flying gallop, will be ready to learn to leap. Indeed, instruction in this accomplishment should always be given, as it is of great assistance in many emergencies. The most gentle horse may become frightened, shy suddenly to one side, or plunge violently for some reason or other, and these abrupt movements strongly resemble those of leaping; if, therefore, the rider understands the leap, she will know better how to maintain her[250] equilibrium. Or she may meet some obstruction on the road, as the trunk of a tree felled by a storm; when, instead of being compelled to return home without finishing her ride, she can leap over the obstacle. Again, should she at any time be in great haste to reach her destination she may, by leaping some low gap in a fence, or some small stream, be able to take one or more short cuts, and thus greatly lessen the distance she would have had to ride on the road.

Leaping is by no means difficult to learn. With an English saddle, the third pommel will prevent the rider from being shaken off by the violence of the motion, and will thus make leaping entirely safe for a lady provided the horse be well-trained and sure-footed. Before venturing upon a leap, three requisites are necessary: first, the horse must be a good and fearless leaper; second, the rider must have confidence in herself and steed, because any nervousness on her part will be apt to cause the animal to leap awkwardly; and third, she must always be sure of the condition of the ground on the opposite side of the object over which the leap is to be made—it must neither slope abruptly down, nor present any thorny bushes, nor be so soft and soggy that the horse will be apt to sink into it. No risk must be taken in the leap, except in cases of emergency, when, of course, the rider may have neither time nor opportunity to select her ground, and be obliged to leap her steed over the nearest available point. The author once avoided what might have proved a serious accident to both herself and horse, by promptly leaping him over a hedge of thorn bushes, upon the other side of which was a river: this was done in order to avoid colliding in a narrow road with a frightened, runaway team, which was quite beyond the control of its driver.

Fig. 33.—The Standing Leap—Rising.

The **standing leap** will prove more difficult to learn than the flying leap, but, nevertheless, it should be the first one practiced, and when once acquired, the other will be mere play. A bar twelve feet long, raised two feet from the ground, will be sufficient for practice in this exercise; if a lady can manage a leap of this height with expertness and grace, she will be fully able to bound over a still higher obstacle, should she desire to do so, and her horse be equal to the occasion. Before attempting the leap, she must be sure that she is perfectly secure upon the saddle, with her left knee directly under the third pommel so as to press it firmly against the latter as the horse rises to the leap;[253]

[254] her left leg, from the knee to the stirrup, must hang perpendicularly[8] along the side of the horse, the inner surface or side of the knee lightly pressing against the saddle-flap; her foot must be well placed in the stirrup; her seat directly in the centre of the saddle; her body erect and square to

the front; her shoulders well back; and the small of her back curved in. The right leg must firmly grasp the second pommel as the horse rises, and the right heel be held somewhat back, and close to the fore-flap of the saddle. The hands must be held low, and about six inches apart, with a snaffle-rein in each, and the curb-reins must be so placed that the rider will not unconsciously draw upon them, but must not hang so loosely as to become caught accidentally upon any projecting article with which they may come in contact. If all these points be carefully attended to, just previous to walking the horse up to the bar, the rider will be in correct position and ready for the leap, which she will accomplish very quickly, with perfect security, and with a much firmer seat than that obtained by the most finished horseman.

[255]

The principal movement for which the rider should be prepared in leaping is that of being thrown forward on the saddle, both when the horse makes the spring and when his fore-feet touch the ground. In order to avoid this accident, the rider, keeping a firm seat and grasp upon the pommels, must incline her shoulders somewhat backward, both when the horse springs from the ground and also during the descent, the amount of inclination varying with the height of the leap. The erect position should be resumed when the hind-legs have again touched the ground. In a very high leap, the rider's body should be bent so far back during the descent as to look almost as if in contact with the back of the horse.

When the points named above have been attended to, the horse must be collected, with his hind-legs well under him, and then be briskly walked up to the bar or obstacle to be leaped and placed directly before it, but not so close that he cannot clear it without striking his knees against it as he rises,—sufficient room must always be allowed him for his spring. Now, after receiving a light touch or pull upon the reins to tell him that his rider is ready, he will raise himself upon his hind-legs for the leap. As he rises, the rider's body, if properly[256] seated, as heretofore explained, will naturally assume a sufficient inclination forward without any effort on her part. While in this position she must not carry her shoulders forward, but must keep them well back, with the waist well curved in as when sitting erect. It should never be forgotten that in the rise during the leap, just previous to the spring, no efforts whatever must be made by the rider to support the horse, or to lift him, but instead, she should simply hold the reins so lightly that his mouth can just be felt, which is called "giving a free rein." If the reins be allowed to hang too loosely they may catch upon some object not noticed by the rider, and not only be wrenched from her hands, but also give the horse's mouth a severe jerk, or perhaps throw him upon the ground. Too loose a rein would, moreover, be apt to make it impossible for her to give timely support to the animal as his fore-feet touched the ground. The leap, it must be borne in mind, is effected very quickly. (Fig. 33.)

As the horse springs from his hind-legs to make the leap, the rider must advance her arms, with her hands held as low as possible so as to give him a sufficiently free rein to enable him to extend himself; this position of the arms will also prevent the reins from being forcibly wrested from her hands by the horse's movements. At the moment of the spring and the advance of the arms, the rider's body must be inclined backward, the erect position of the waist and shoulders being, however, maintained. As the animal's fore-feet touch the ground, the hands must be gently drawn in toward the waist in order to support him, as such support will be expected by the horse, and must be continued even after his hind-legs rest upon the ground, so that the animal will not become disunited, but will move onward in a collected manner. (Fig. 34.)

Fig. 34.—The Standing Leap—Descending.

Many riding-teachers instruct their pupils to incline the body well forward as the horse rises, while others require their pupils to lean well back. The advocates of the former method say that this forward inclination conforms to the position of the horse at the time, and so places the weight of the body as to assist the horse in his spring. They who adopt the other method maintain that if the body be inclined forward in the rise, it will be almost, if not quite, impossible for the rider, from the rapidity with which the horse extends himself, to make the backward inclination in time to enable her to regain her balance quickly. A happy medium will prove the best. If the rider be seated correctly[259]

[260] at the time the horse rises, her body *will naturally incline a little forward*, and there will be but little

weight upon the horse's hind-quarters, while, as he springs and extends himself in his leap, she can promptly adapt herself to his movements and incline her body backward.

By leaning back as the horse rises on his hind-legs, the weight of his rider will be thrown upon his hind-quarters, and she will present an awkward appearance; while at the same time she will be very apt to shorten the reins, and thus confine the horse so much that his leap will become clumsy and dangerous.

On commencing the leap the rider, as heretofore stated, must never attempt to raise the horse by the reins; a light, gentle touch or pull given to them with the fingers, as when starting upon a hand gallop, is all that will be necessary. The horse must be left free to take the leap in his own way, using his own instinct or judgment in order that he may clear his fore feet from the bar or object over which he has to pass. During the rise, the rider must carefully guard against raising her hands, and also against jerking or holding back the reins, as either of these movements will discourage the horse, and, should he be tender mouthed, he[261] will refuse to leap at all, his own instinct warning him that it is dangerous to attempt it under such conditions.

A rather hard mouthed, courageous animal, that has had experience with awkward riders, will, as he extends himself in the leap, force his rider's hands by a sudden jerk of his head, so as either to pull the reins out of her hands, or, should she manage to retain her hold upon them, to pull her forward upon the saddle.

Many ladies, in their fear of becoming displaced during the leap, will unconsciously press their left leg and foot strongly against the side of the horse, thus causing him to swerve or to refuse to leap. Gentlemen teachers are apt to be unaware of this pressure, as the leg is hidden underneath the riding skirt, and not unfrequently they have been puzzled to comprehend why a well-trained, docile horse should leap very well with some of their lady pupils, and awkwardly, or not at all, with others.

A common error, in attempting to leap, is to sit too far back upon the saddle, a position that not only prevents the rider from supporting herself properly by the pommels, but is also likely to occasion her a severe jar as the horse's feet touch the ground. When in the correct position, the body is placed as far forward upon[262] the saddle as the pommels will permit, the waist and shoulders only being inclined backward, as already described.

Pressing heavily upon the stirrup is another fault. This not only destroys the usefulness of the third pommel, but, as has already been remarked, such pressure will tend to lift the body from the saddle. The foot should merely be kept light and steady in the stirrup.

It will be better for a beginner to leap with a snaffle-rein in each hand. After having thoroughly learned how to make the leap properly, she may then prefer to hold all the reins in the left hand. In this case, she must be very careful not to throw up the unoccupied right hand and arm as the horse passes over the obstacle; for, besides being a very ungraceful movement, it may lead the horse to suppose that he is about to be struck with the whip, and so cause him to make the leap precipitately, and upon reaching the ground to gallop wildly off.

The rider must hold her head firm, not only for the sake of appearances, but also to escape biting her tongue and receiving a violent jerk of the neck, when the horse's feet touch the ground.

If a horse, just before leaping, be too much confined or collected by an unnecessary degree[263] of tension upon the reins, especially if he be not thoroughly trained, he will rise from all four legs almost simultaneously, and also alight upon them all together. In horse-jockey's *parlance* this is termed a "buck-leap." It is an awkward manner of leaping, and gives a severe shock to the animal beside fearfully jolting his rider. Again, a horse not well trained in the leap, or somewhat indolent, may, if not animated and properly collected just before rising, fail to leap over the obstacle, or in passing over it may strike it with his hind-feet, for he will attempt the leap in a loose, straggling manner. An animal that is well trained, and accustomed to leaping, will take care of himself, and will require very little assistance from his rider; a light hand upon the reins just before he rises, a free rein as he extends himself, and support when he touches the ground being all that is necessary.

Should the lady be expert in riding, and desire to teach her steed to leap, she can readily do so by pursuing the following course: Let a bar about twelve feet in length, and two feet from the ground, be so arranged that the horse cannot pass around it. If possible, he should be allowed to see a well-trained horse leap over this bar a number of times; then taking advantage[264] of a time when her horse is hungry, his mistress should give him a few oats and, passing over the bar, she should rattle the oats and call to him, when he will bound over to obtain them. This course should be followed at each meal, and she should reward him by feeding, caressing, and praising him every time he leaps the bar,—the object being to accustom him to leap it without being whipped or treated harshly. By thus being allowed to take the leap of his own accord and without assistance, he will gain confidence, and will not be apt to refuse when his rider is placed upon his back. In the course of this training, the appearance of the bar should be changed in various ways, as, for example, by placing different bright colored articles upon it, such as pieces of carpet, rugs, shawls, etc. If he be accustomed to leap only over an object that invariably presents the same appearance, he may refuse to leap one of a different aspect.

Having thus trained the horse until he has become quite familiar with the movements of the leap, and does not refuse to pass over the bar, whatever appearance it may present, he will then be ready for his rider. For the first few trials the lady should take care to have the bar consist of some material that can readily be[265] broken, in order to prevent any accident should the horse, in passing over with her weight upon his back, strike it with either his fore or hind feet. Once mounted, she should teach him to clear the bar in a deliberate manner, not allowing him to rush at it and jump from all four feet at once. She will have to collect him, cause him to place his hind-legs under him so that, as he rises, his weight will be thrown upon his haunches, and, as he leaps over, she must be exceedingly careful not to restrain him in the least, as any thoughtless act or awkwardness on her part may give him a great distaste for an exercise which, otherwise, he would have no reluctance in performing.

With regard to teaching a young horse to leap, the author is much gratified to know that her views are sustained by several eminent equestrians, and among them Mr. E. Mayhew of England, who states that a horse should never be allowed to leap until he has attained at least his fifth year, and who in his excellent work, entitled "The Illustrated Horse Management," etc., remarks: "To place a rider upon an animal's back and then to expect a bar to be cleared is very like loading a young lady with a sack of flour, as preparatory to a dancing lesson being received. This folly is, however, universally[266] practiced; so is that of teaching the paces, when the quadruped's attention is probably engrossed by the burden which the spine has to sustain.

"Leaping is best taught by turning the horse into a small paddock having a low hedge or hurdle-fence across its centre. A rider should, in sight of the animal, take an old horse over several times. The groom who brings the corn at the meal hour then goes to that side where the animal is not and calls, shaking up the provender all the time his voice sounds. The boundary will soon be cleared. When half the quantity is eaten, the man should proceed to the opposite compartment and call again. If this is done every time the young horse is fed, the fence may be gradually heightened; after six months of such tuition, a light rider may be safely placed upon the back.

"Instruction, thus imparted, neither strains the structures nor tries the temper. The habit is acquired without those risks which necessarily attend a novel performance, while a burden oppresses the strength, and whip or spur distracts the attention. The body is not disabled by the imposition of a heavy load before its powers are taxed to the uttermost. The quadruped has all its capabilities unfettered, and, in such a state,[267]leaping speedily becomes as easy of performance as any other motion."

Horses leap in different ways; the best leapers being those which just glide over the object without touching it,—they appear to measure the height required for the leap, and, whether the object be high or low, they skim close to it. Such animals can be trusted, and may be allowed to leap without urging or hurrying them, for they require very little assistance from their riders, and do better when left to themselves. Other horses exaggerate the leap and rise higher than is required; they make a very fine appearance when leaping, but are apt to light too close to the opposite side of the bar or obstacle, because they expend all their energies on height instead of width. The worst leapers are those which, instead of clearing the bar at a single bound, make two bounds, as it were, in passing over it: the fore-part of the horse having passed over, the body will seem to be resting for an appreciable time upon the fore-legs.

The **flying leap** can be taken, without stopping, from any gait that is more rapid than a walk, though commonly taken from the gallop. It is a very easy leap, being little more than an extended gallop. The rider takes the same firm, central position upon the saddle as has been described[268] for the standing leap. In the flying leap the body must be inclined well back from the start, care being taken not to make any forward inclination whatever. When the horse has fairly landed, after the leap, the body must again become erect. The degree of the backward inclination must be in accordance with the height and width of the leap. During the whole period of the leap the hands must be kept low and the reins be freely given to the animal, which must be supported as he lands on the opposite side. As the horse runs toward the object to be leaped over, the rider must, when about twelve or fifteen yards from it, gradually relax the reins, by advancing her bridle hand or hands; and, if her horse be a willing and good leaper, he may be allowed to select his own pace, and use his own judgment as to the proper distance from which to make the spring.

If the horse be unused to leaping, or be unwilling, the rider must be upon her guard lest he attempt to defend himself and avoid the leap, either by suddenly swerving to one side or by stopping before the object to be leaped and then backing, or rearing. These actions are generally the result of the horse's want of confidence in his own powers, and severity will only make matters worse. In a dilemma of this kind, the [269] rider will have to convert the flying into the standing leap, as follows:—

She must turn her horse and walk him a short distance away from the object, then, turning him again toward it, she must encourage him to advance slowly that he may take a good look at it; at the same time she must have a light and ready hand on the reins, just firm enough to keep his head steady and maintain control over his neck, so as to prevent him from swerving to the right or to the left. She should then kindly and firmly encourage him to make the bound; and by patience and perseverance in this course he will generally be induced to do so. After he has obeyed, she must not make him repeat the movement several times in succession, as if she were triumphing over him, because he might regard such a process as a sort of challenge, and renew the contest; instead of such measures, he should be allowed to pass on quietly, no further attention being given to the matter. By this change from the flying to the standing leap the horse can be better prevented from shying, and on the next occasion will be apt to make the flying leap over the object without swerving.

The whip or spur should never be employed to make an obstinate or timid horse leap, as he will ever after associate such objects as those [270] over which he has been thus urged or forced to leap with fear of punishment, and his rider will never be sure of him when approaching one of them, for he will either shy, or else bound over it in such a flurried manner as will prove dangerous both to himself and his rider. An indolent horse, that requires to be roused by whip or spur, is not a suitable one for a lady to ride at a leap. Some horses will refuse to leap when traveling alone, but will do so spiritedly and excellently when in company with others of their kind.

[271]

CHAPTER XII.
DEFENSES OF THE HORSE.—CRITICAL SITUATIONS.

"High pampered steeds, ere tamed, the lash disdain,
And proudly foam, impatient of the rein."

VIRGIL, *Sotheby's Translation.*

"The startling steed was seized with sudden fright."

DRYDEN.

A lady's horse is generally selected for his gentleness, soundness, good training, and freedom from vice, and the rider's management of him is usually so kind and considerate that he is seldom roused to rebellion; hence, she is rarely called upon to enter into a contention with him. The docility of a lady's steed is almost proverbial, and when purchasing a horse the highest recommendation as to his gentleness and safeness is the assurance that he has "been used to carry a woman." Horse-dealers are well acquainted with this fact, and attach a high value to it, as a sure criterion of the animal's kindly nature. No lady rider, however expert she may be, will, if she be wise and have a regard for her own safety, ride or endeavor to conquer a really vicious horse; yet there [272] may be times when even the hitherto most docile animal will suddenly display that which in Yorkshire dialect is called "mistech;" that is, there may be unexpectedly developed a restive trait, for which there seems to be no reason. Even a really good-natured horse may, owing to high feed and little work, shy, plunge, and kick, in his exuberance of spirits, and should his rider not know how to control these sudden and unexpected manifestations, he may gain the ascendency, and she be thrown from the saddle. That which, on the part of the horse, is intended for good-humored play, may thus, from want of control, degenerate into positive viciousness. A skillful rider will manage and endure the prancings, pawings, and impatience of her steed,—which are frequently only his method of expressing satisfaction and happiness in carrying his kind mistress,—and will continue riding and controlling him until he becomes calm and quiet, and ceases to display his impulsive sensitiveness. Again, a lady may have occasion to ride a strange horse, of whose disposition she knows very little. It is, therefore, very important that every horsewoman should be prepared to meet and to overcome any eccentric demonstrations on the part of the animal she may be riding.

[273]

Some horses are constitutionally nervous and timid, always fearful and upon the lookout, constantly scrutinizing every object around them, and keeping their riders incessantly on the watch. These horses, though disagreeable to ride, are seldom dangerous, as they will readily obey the reins and yield to the hand that has many times proved its reliability and correctness.

SHYING.—The position in which a horse places his ears is a sure indication of his immediate intentions. When he raises his head and points his ears strongly forward, it is because he sees some object at the side of the road, or approaching, which renders him uneasy or even fearful. In such a case, his rider must be prepared for a sudden leap to one side, a whirl around, or a quick darting from the road. She must not allow herself to become nervous and jerk or suddenly tighten the reins, for then the animal will think that she is likewise afraid, and that he is justified in his own fright. On the contrary, she must maintain her presence of mind, quietly and calmly take a snaffle-rein in each hand, draw them just tight enough to feel the horse's mouth, keep his head high and straight forward, and, as he approaches the object that has alarmed him, gently turn his head[274] away from it, so that in passing he can see as little of it as possible; at the same time she should press her leg or whip against the horse on the side toward which he is likely to shy,—also speaking to him in a firm and assuring tone of voice, that he may be led to understand there is nothing to fear.

In following these directions the rider must be mindful of her balance, because, notwithstanding all her efforts, the horse may leap out of the road; she should sit erect, keep a firm hold on both pommels with the legs, check him as soon as possible, and then bring him again upon the road. Should he swerve and attempt to rush past the object, his rider must not try to pull his head toward it, but, holding the reins with steady hands, must keep him headed straight forward, and, after he has passed, gradually rein him in.

Should he make a half turn from the object, he must be turned completely around, so as to face it, and then be urged forward by the aid of the left leg and whip, while he is at the same time spoken to in a quiet, encouraging tone. If the horse have confidence in his rider, and his fright be not a pretense, he will thus be induced to go by, and on future occasions will pass by the same object with indifference. Severity,[275] such as scolding and whipping, will only render him more fearful, and since he will always regard the object of his fright as being the cause of his punishment, he will, consequently, the next time of meeting with it become still more unmanageable. But, having passed it at first without experiencing any pain, he will gain confidence in the judgment of his rider, imagine he has made a mistake in being alarmed, and be satisfied that, after all, there was no occasion for dread.

A horse should never be caressed, patted, or coaxed, either just before or just after he has passed any object he dislikes, because he may misinterpret these acts, and imagine that he has done just right in shying, and will, therefore, be very apt to repeat the act in order again to receive the praise of his rider. It will always be better, in such cases, to ride on as usual, and act as if the matter were of no consequence. On the other hand, a horse should never be whipped after he has passed an object that terrifies him. Some riders are afraid to whip the horse while he is in the act of shying, but will lay on the lash after he has passed the cause of his dread; this will not only be "a tardy vengeance that crowns a cowardly act," but will cause the animal to conclude that he[276] has done wrong in passing by, and on the next occasion for alarm he will either delay as long as possible in dread of the remembered whipping, or else will plunge quickly by the object, and, perhaps, add to the vice of shying that of running away. The course pursued by some persons of making a horse pass and repass a number of times in succession an object which has caused him to shy is an erroneous one, as it gives him a chance for again resisting, and makes the rider appear vainglorious and pretentious.

Whether a horse shies from real fright, or from mere pretense or affectation, the severe use of whip or spur to force him by the object he is shying at will always do more harm than good. Mildness and forbearance, combined with firmness, will invariably do much more to tranquillize him and to render him obedient than severity and harsh measures. Horsemen who, from actual experience, are well able to advise say, "Let the horse alone, neither letting him perceive that we are aware we are advancing toward anything that he dislikes, nor doing more with him when in the act of shying than is necessary for due restraint and a steady hand upon the reins."

When a horse shies from pretense of fright,[277] it is either from exuberance of spirits, because he has not been sufficiently exercised, or else because he has detected timidity in his rider, and shies from pure love of mischief and the desire to amuse himself by augmenting her fears. Although not intending any real harm, he may manage, to his own astonishment, to unseat her, and, by thus discovering what he can do, may become a vicious rogue, and make every strange object an excuse for a dangerous shy. The only remedy for this affectation and mischievousness will be a courageous and determined rider on his back, who will give him more work than he likes; he will then, of his own accord, soon tire of his tricks.

When a horse that has had plenty of work and a good rider to manage him nevertheless continues to shy, it will generally be found that his vision is defective. If he is a young horse, with very prominent eyes, the probability is that he is near-sighted; if an old horse, that his vision—having undergone a change similar to that of a human being who is advanced in years—is imperfect for near objects, which appear confused and blurred; in other words, that he is troubled with long-sightedness, or presbyopia. In these cases the horse becomes fearful and suspicious, and his quick imagination[278] transforms that which he cannot distinctly see into something terrifying. Ocular science has not advanced so far as to have determined a remedy for these visual difficulties except by the use of glasses; and to place spectacles upon a horse to improve his sight would be inconvenient as well as decidedly unique. Animals thus afflicted are unsuited for either saddle or harness, as they are more dangerous than if they are totally blind, and the only safe course to pursue when one is compelled to use them will be the very undesirable one of completely blindfolding them. Many a horse has been severely punished and condemned for viciousness, when his fault arose from defective vision.

Sometimes a horse becomes discontented and uneasy from being always ridden over the same road; this dull routine is irksome to him, especially if he be spirited, and he ventures upon some act of disobedience in order to create variety and excitement. He may commence by sideling toward other horses or objects on his left, or by suddenly turning around to the right. In the first case, the rider must instantly take a snaffle-rein in each hand, and instead of attempting to turn him from the object, she must rein his head directly toward it, and then back him from it. By these means, his body will form a[279] concavity on the side toward the object, thus preventing injury to the rider or horse, and she will be able to retreat in safety.

In the second instance, the horse instinctively knows that he is opposing his strongest side to the weakest one of his rider, and it is useless to contend with him by pulling upon the left snaffle-rein, as he will be watching for this very movement and be prepared to resist it. He should be foiled by having the right rein tightened so as to turn him completely around and place him in the same position he was in before he began to turn. He will perceive to his astonishment that he has gained nothing by his abrupt movement; and as soon as he has reached the position stated, he should be urged forward by the aid of both leg and whip.

This method is usually successful unless the steed be very obstinate; he may then refuse to advance at all, and may make another turn to the right, in which case his rider should repeat the course just named, and oblige him to turn completely around three or four times in succession, and then while his head is in the right direction, a stroke of the whip behind the girths should instantly be given in order to compel him to go forward before he has time to defend himself and make another turn. Should he again[280] refuse, and succeed in making still another turn, the tactics of his rider must be changed; taking care not to use her whip, she must turn him around as before, and then rein him backward in the direction she desires him to go; she must keep doing this until he concludes to move onward. Should this course have to be continued for some time, it will be advisable occasionally to head him in the desired direction, in order to ascertain whether he will go forward; if he will not, he must again be turned and backed. A horse can readily be induced to move backward, when he has determined not to go forward.

During this contest with the horse, the rider must be careful to retain her balance, to keep her left knee directly under the third pommel, and to incline her body quickly to the right as her animal turns. She should likewise be watchful of surrounding objects, in order to protect herself and her horse from any dangerous position in which he may be disposed to place himself. In case she is not a very expert horsewoman, or has little confidence in her ability to manage the horse, it will be better to have him led a short distance, and then, if possible, she should change the road to one he has not been accustomed to travel; this will divert him, and cause him to forget his contumacy.

[281]

BALKING.—When a horse stops on the road and refuses to move in any direction, it may be owing to disease (immobility), or to obstinacy. In either case, it will be better for the rider to make no effort to induce him to move, but she should quietly and patiently remain in the saddle until he evinces a disposition to advance, when he should be made to stand a little longer. If his defense be due to obstinacy, this course will be a punishment; but should it be due to disease, the detention will be no disadvantage nor punishment to him, but rather an advantage, as it will enable him to gain composure. It is rarely, however, that a horse proves balky, unless as the result of some disease of the brain or of the heart, rheumatic pain, etc.

BACKING.—Should a horse commence backing, when on the road, he must have his head quickly turned toward the direction in which he is backing. Thus, if he be backing toward a dangerous declivity, he will be able to see that what he is doing threatens danger to himself, and will be checked. Then he must be backed some little distance away from the danger, and in the direction toward which he is desired to go. If, however, the horse continues to back toward the dangerous place, notwithstanding the rider's efforts to turn him, the safest course[282] will be to dismount instantly. Backing is sometimes, if not very frequently, due to confused vision, rush of blood to the head, pain in the head, etc.

GAYETY.—When a horse moves one ear back and forth, or keeps agitating first one and then the other, at the same time moving his head and neck up and down, and, perhaps, also champing upon his bit, he is feeling gay, and his rider must be on her guard, as he may unexpectedly jump. While keeping a steady hand upon the reins, she must urge him to move forward at a regular and somewhat rapid gait, for this will be what he wants in order to work off his superfluous spirits.

KICKING.—A horse, when defending himself against anything whatever, will always lay his ears flat upon the back of his head; this is his attitude and signal for a battle, and he is then ready to kick, bite, plunge, or rear. When the ears are only momentarily placed back, it may be from playfulness, but when maintained in this position, he is angry and vicious, and may make a desperate effort to throw his rider. In the company of other horses he will attempt to bite or kick at them. As soon as he is observed to gaze fixedly upon any animals in his vicinity, while at the same time he puts his ears back,[283] and turns his croup toward his companions, he is then about to kick, and his rider must frustrate his intention, as soon as she feels his croup move, by quickly raising his head and turning it in the direction in which the kick was to be made. Should he attempt to bite, he must be driven to a proper distance from the object of his anger, and his attention be diverted by keeping him moving on.

A horse will kick when feeling gay, when he is annoyed, when he suffers pain from any cause, when feeling playful or malevolent toward other animals, and, sometimes, when he wishes to dislodge his rider. Whenever her horse manifests an inclination to kick, the rider must endeavor to keep his head up, because he will then be unable to accomplish much in the way of raising his hind-legs; but once allowed to get his head down, he will have everything his own way, and will be able to kick as high as he pleases.

Every time the horse attempts to lower his head, he must be punished by a pull upon the curb-bit strong enough to make him keep his head up. His mouth must also be sawed upon with the curb, should he succeed in getting his head down. The rider must remember to lean well back, and have her left knee well braced against the third pommel, as in this position it[284] will be almost impossible for him to unseat her by his kicking. If the kick be made during a stand-still, a sharp, vigorous stroke of the whip upon the animal's shoulder will be apt to check him; but if the kick be made while he is on the gallop, a stroke of the whip will be apt to make him run away. Should kicking be an old vice of the horse, he must be ridden with a severe curb-bit, that he may be prevented from getting his head down.

PLUNGING, BUCKING.—Plunging is a succession of bounds, in which the four legs of the horse are almost simultaneously raised from the ground, the animal advancing with each bound. It is frequently an effort made by the horse to rid himself of something that pains him, as the sting of an insect, the pinching of the saddle or the girth, etc. All that can be done in any case of plunging will be to endeavor to keep up the animal's head, brace one's self firmly in the saddle, and sit the plunges out; they will rarely amount to more than three or four. When a horse that is not vicious commences to plunge, it may be due to fear or pain; he should, therefore, be spoken to kindly, and be soothed. As soon as he is brought under control, the rider should endeavor to ascertain the cause of his movements, and, if possible, remove it.

[285]

Bucking is a desperate effort to throw the rider; the horse will gather his legs under him in as close a group as possible, curve his back upward like an angry Tabby when she espies Towser, lower his head, endeavor to burst the saddle-girths by forcibly expanding his abdomen, and then without making any advance or retreat bound up and down upon all four legs, which are held as rigid as iron rods. Sometimes he will produce a see-saw movement by repeatedly and rapidly throwing himself from his hind to his fore legs. These motions will be kept up as long as he can hold his breath, which generally becomes exhausted after five or six bounds; he will then renew his breath and may repeat the bounds.

When a horse "bucks," the rider must keep her seat the best way she can. Her body should be held as straight as possible, although the natural tendency will be to lean forward and to round the shoulders; she should also take a firm knee-grasp upon both the second and third pommels, keep a steady hold upon the reins, and be especially on her guard against allowing her body to be pulled forward as the horse jerks his head down. Fortunately, very few thorough-bred horses buck violently, their movement being more of a plunge. The horses of the[286] Russian steppes, and the bronchos and ponies of our far Western country, are apt to have the vicious, genuine buck in perfection.

REARING.—With the young horse, rearing is the last frantic effort to unseat his rider; an old rogue will sometimes resort to it, having found his rider timid and much alarmed at the movement. A lady should never ride a horse that has once reared dangerously, unless the action was occasioned by the injudicious use of too severe a curb-bit. A horse that has once reared without provocation will be very apt to do so again. The danger of this vice is, that the horse may fall backward and upon his rider. This accident will be especially liable to occur when, in rearing suddenly and very high, he bends his fore-legs under his body. While he is in this position, should the rider feel him sinking down upon his hind-quarters, she must instantly leap from the saddle, at the same time giving, if possible, a vigorous push to the horse with both hands, as near his shoulder as she can readily reach without endangering herself. This is done that he may be made to fall to the right, and the impetus of the push will also convey her to a safe distance, should he fall to the left.

When a horse, after rearing, paws in the air with his fore-feet, he is then employing them[287] for the same purpose that a tight-rope dancer uses his balancing pole, namely, to keep his equilibrium. In this case, there will not be much danger of his falling backward, unless his rider should pull him over by holding too tight a rein, or by using the reins to aid her in keeping her balance.

The first act of the horse, when he intends to rear, will be to free himself from the influence of the bit, and he will attempt to accomplish this by bending his neck in so as to slacken the tension on the reins; at the same time he will come to a stand by a peculiar cringing movement, which will make his rider feel as if the animal had collapsed, or were falling to pieces. This "nowhere" feeling will hardly be realized before the horse will stiffen his hind-legs and neck, and rise with his fore-feet in the air, bidding defiance to all control.

Under these circumstances, as the horse rears his rider must quickly yield the reins and incline her body well forward, firmly supporting herself by the second and third pommels; as she values her life, she must not strike her steed nor pull upon the reins, but must patiently wait until his fore-feet come to the ground, when the time for action will have arrived.

Although she may be taken by surprise when[288] the horse first rears, she can anticipate his second attempt, which will generally be not far off, by taking a snaffle-rein in each hand, holding her hands low, and the instant she perceives that he is going to rise, loosening the left rein and tightening the right, so as to bend his head to the right. He cannot now complete the rear, because her action will compel him to move a hind-leg, and he will then be unable to rest his weight upon both hind-legs, which he must do in order to rear. As a punishment, he should then be turned around a few times, from right to left; this turning will also be very apt to prevent him from again rearing. Sometimes a severe stroke with the whip upon the horse's hind-quarters as his fore-feet are descending to the ground will prevent the second rear; as he plunges forward from the whip, the rider must be careful to prevent her body from being thrown forward by the plunge.

RUNNING AWAY.—The most dangerous runaway horse is the one that starts off from excessive fear, as terror will make a horse act as if he were blind, and he may then rush over a precipice, or violently collide with some object in his way. Terrified horses have been known almost to dash out their brains by violent collision with a stone wall, and even to impale themselves[289] upon an iron fence. The least dangerous runaway steed is the practiced one, which runs because he has vicious propensities; for as he knows what he is about, he generally takes good care of himself, and thus, in a measure, protects his rider, of whose mishaps, however, he is entirely regardless. Some horses, when urged to do something that is beyond their ability, or when goaded by pain from any cause, will run, imagining that by so doing they can escape the evil. With these, the "bolt" or runaway is more the last furious effort of despair than real viciousness. A heavy-handed rider may cause a horse to run away, the horse, taking advantage of the constant pull upon the reins, is liable to make the hand of his rider a point of support, and then dash wildly onward.

When, from restlessness, a horse endeavors to break away, the curb-reins should be taken, one in each hand, and every time he attempts to run, a sharp pull should be made upon his mouth by means of these reins; he will thus be checked and prevented from starting upon a run. Should he once get fairly started, it will be very difficult to stop him promptly. In such a case, care should be taken not to make a "dead pull" upon the reins, but instead, a succession of pulls at short intervals, and these efforts should[290] be continued until he comes to a stand; should the horse manifest any disposition to stop, the rider should, as he slackens his speed, make a continued pull on the reins as if reining him in from the walk, and this will gradually check him.

When a horse runs away from fear or pain, nothing will stop him except the voice of the rider in whom he has confidence, and for whom he entertains affection. In his terror, he will rely entirely upon her for aid and support, and if she fail him, the most severe bit will not stop him. An old offender may sometimes be controlled by a severe bit, or may be cured of his propensity for running by being placed in the hands of a good horseman who will allow him to run away, and when the animal wishes to stop, will then, by means of whip and spur, make him run still farther, and allow him to stop only when the rider pleases.

The management of a horse when he attempts to "bolt" has been described in the chapter on the Hand Gallop. A horse that has once fairly run away and met with some catastrophe, or that has thrown his rider, will never be a safe one to ride subsequently.

UNSTEADINESS WHILE BEING MOUNTED.—It is very annoying, as well as dangerous, to have a horse moving about unsteadily while the rider[291] is attempting to mount; this restlessness is sometimes occasioned by his impatience and eagerness to start, and may then be remedied by having him held by the bit, with his right side placed against a wall, fence, or other firm barrier, where he can be kept until the lady has mounted. The horse must not be allowed to start immediately after the rider has become seated, but must be restrained until he is perfectly quiet, and must be chidden every time he commences to prance. A few lessons of this kind will teach him to stand still while being mounted.

When the horse from viciousness, or from dislike to carrying a rider, attempts to evade being mounted, he had better be disposed of; for should the lady succeed in mounting she will receive but little benefit from the ride, as the bad temper and unwillingness of her steed will not only make it unpleasant, but even dangerous for her.

Sometimes the restiveness of the horse may be the fault of the person holding him, who, perhaps, either takes too heavy a hold of the snaffle-rein, thus pressing the sides of the snaffle-bit against the animal's mouth, and pinching him, or pulls upon the curb-reins, which should not be touched. Either of these mistakes will cause the horse to move backward. Not unfrequently[292] a horse will violently plunge and kick from the pain of some injury in his side or back, which, though not painful when the rider is seated, becomes so when she bears upon the stirrup. Such a horse is unsound and not suitable for a side-saddle.

STUMBLING.—When a horse, not naturally indolent, and having his ears well placed, allows the latter to project out and to fall loosely on each side of his head, he is then fatigued, and must be kept well supported by the bridle, for he may stumble, or even fall. Whenever a horse is felt to trip or stumble, the rider's body must instantly be inclined backward, her hands be lifted, and her horse be steadied and supported by sufficient tension on the reins. Should the tired horse be walking down a hill, he must always be well balanced by pressure of both leg and whip; this will keep him light upon his fore-legs, and he will not be so apt to fall.

A horse should never be whipped for stumbling, as it is not likely that he would do so of his own accord, and it would be cruel to punish the poor animal for what he could not help. It may be the fault of the blacksmith in not shoeing him properly.

Should an indolent horse fail to raise his feet sufficiently to escape tripping, the proper course[293] to pursue will be to keep him collected and make him move at rather a rapid gait, because, when he is animated, he will lift his feet more briskly and to better advantage.

A straight-shouldered horse, when carrying a woman, will be apt to stumble, to bear upon the reins, and to move heavily on his fore-feet, and will therefore require an expert horsewoman to keep him moving in good form.

When the rider hears a metallic clinking sound at each step of her horse, it will be an indication that the shoes of his hind-feet are striking against those of his fore-feet; this is very dangerous, as in the trot, or gallop, he may "overreach" and strike one of his fore-legs with one of his hind-shoes in such a manner as to injure himself severely, or he may catch the toe of a hind-shoe in the heel of a fore-shoe so that they will become locked together, when the fore-shoe will have to give way and come off, or a terrific fall will ensue. Some horses overreach on account of their natural conformation, others only when fatigued; again, some will be free from this defect when fat, but will manifest it when they become lean from overwork, deficiency of food, or other cause. Young horses will occasionally move in this manner before they are taught their paces, but as soon as they[294] are thoroughly trained this dangerous annoyance ceases.

When a horse falls to the ground, or merely falls on his knees, if the rider be not thrown off by the violence of the shock it will be better for her to keep to the saddle, as the horse will rise very quickly, and if she attempts to jump off he may step upon her as he is in the act of rising, or her habit may catch upon the pommel and add to the peril of the situation by causing her to be dragged along should the horse move on, or become frightened and run away. She must not attempt to assist the horse by pulling upon the bridle, but must allow him to get upon his feet in his own way. Should she be thrown off as he falls, she must free her skirt from the saddle as promptly as possible and quickly get away from him in order to escape being stepped upon as he rises. The fall of a horse upon his right side is much less dangerous than upon his left, because in the latter case the rider's left leg may be caught beneath him, perhaps injured, and she would then be unable to extricate herself without assistance.

WHIP AND SPUR.—A lady's whip is employed as a substitute for the right leg of the horseman in collecting and guiding the horse. For this reason, it must always be firm, strong, and well-made.[295] It is also used both to give light taps to the horse in order to increase his speed, and likewise, when necessary, to chastise him moderately and thus make him more obedient. If it can possibly be avoided, a lady should never whip her horse; but when it is required, one quick, sharp stroke, given at the right time, and with judgment, will subdue him and bring him to his senses. Deliberately to give stroke after stroke, or to flog him, will always do more harm than good, for it will make him wild, vicious, and unmanageable, and the lady will gain nothing by it except the reputation of being a *virago.*

When a horse has committed a fault requiring the whip, he knows that the first stroke given is for this fault, and submits; but he does not understand why the succeeding blows are given, and resents them accordingly. An expert rider will rarely whip her horse, and will never become angry at even the most obstinate resistance on his part, but will, instead, manage him intelligently, and subdue him in a subtle way that he cannot comprehend. She will turn his disobedient acts against himself in a manner that is mysterious to him, and which will make them appear to him to be the will of his rider. The horse will find himself foiled at every turn, in a way against which he can present no permanent[296] defense, and there will be nothing left for him but submission.

When a horse fails in his attempts to gain the ascendency, and yields to her skill and authority, she should be generous and forgiving, and treat the vanquished one with kindness and consideration, letting him know that there is no resentment harbored against him. He will quickly appreciate this forbearance, and it will have a lasting effect. But while accepting the olive branch, she should not give him his usual pats and caresses for some little while afterward, as these acts might be misinterpreted by him as a weakening on the part of his rider, or lead him to imagine that he has been doing right instead of wrong.

A lady's horse should never be trained with the spur. The horse that requires a spur is unsuited for the side-saddle; even the dullest animal will soon learn that he is spurred only on one side, and will shrink from the attack by a shy or a jump to the right, knowing there is no spur on this side. An indifferent rider may place herself in danger by unconsciously spurring her horse, thus goading him to madness, and to such a frenzy of despair that the only alternative left for him will be to unseat his fair rider in order to escape the pain thus unconsciously inflicted upon him.

[297]

The novice in riding must not be dismayed nor discouraged by all the instructions in regard to defending one's self against restive and vicious horses, as she may ride for years, or even for a life-time, and never be in any serious danger. But a time might possibly come, when she would suddenly and unexpectedly be called upon to exert herself in order to exact obedience from her steed, or to extricate herself from a perilous situation, and then a knowledge of what should be done will be of great use to her. Being armed at all points, and understanding the means required for any emergency, she will not depend for safety altogether upon the caprice or the gentleness of her horse, but chiefly upon her own knowledge and skill; this will give her a confidence and sense of security that will greatly add to the pleasure of her ride.

[298]

View larger image.

EXPLANATION.

. The lips.

. Tip of the nose. Figs. 1 and 2 form the muzzle.

. Chanfrin, or face; the parts that correspond to the bones of the nose, and that extend from the brow to the nostrils.

. The brow, or forehead.

. The eye-pits; cavities more or less deeply situated above the eyes.

. Forelock; hairs between the ears that fall upon the forehead.

. The ears.

. The lower jaw and channel, or space comprised between the two lower jaws. Cheek. Jowl.

. The jaws: nether jaws.

0. The nostril.

1. The throat.

2. Region of parotid glands, at the posterior and internal part of each of the lower-jaw bones.

3. The crest.

3′. The mane.

4. Windpipe and groove of the jugular veins.

5. The chest, thorax.

6. The withers, or the sharp, projecting part at the inferior extremity of the crest and of the mane. It is formed by the projection of the first dorsal vertebra.

7. The back, or part upon which the saddle is placed.

8. The ribs.

9. The passage for the girths.

0. The loins.

1. The croup; the most elevated part of the posterior extremity of the body.

2. The tail.

4. The flank.

5. The abdomen.

7. The saphena vein.

8. The shoulder and arm.

The point of the shoulder.

8′.

9. The elbow.

0. The fore-arm.

2. The knee.

3. The cannon bone, shank.

4. The large pastern joint.

5. The small pastern joint.

6. The coronet.

7. The front foot and hoof.

8. The fetlock and ergot. The fetlock consists of hairs, and the ergot of a horny-like substance constantly found at the back and lower part of the large pastern joints.

9. The haunch.

0. The thigh, gaskin, or femur.

1. The stifle joint.

2. The buttock.

3. The tibia, or leg proper (lower thigh); a small bone lies behind it, the *fibula.*

4. The hock (curb place).

4′. The point of the hock.

6. The cannon bone.

7. The large pastern joint.

8. The fetlock and ergot.

9. The small pastern joint.

0. The coronet.

1. Hind-foot and hoof.

ADDENDA.

GOOD RULES TO BE REMEMBERED.

(1.) When in company with a gentleman, an accomplished horsewoman will prefer to have him ride at the right side of her horse, because, being thoroughly able to control her steed, she will require little or no assistance from the cavalier. On the contrary, if she be an inexperienced rider, it will be better for the gentleman to ride at the left side, because, in this position, his right hand will be free to render any assistance she may require, and he will also be placed between her and any approaching object.

(2.) A finished horseman, when riding at the left side of a lady's horse, will not allow his spurs to catch in her dress, nor will he permit his steed to press so closely against this left side as to injure or interfere with the action of her left foot and leg.

(3.) In the park, or in any public place, a gentleman should always approach a lady on the off-side of her horse.

(4.) When in company with two ladies, a gentleman should ride on the off-side of them, and never between the two, unless they request it.

(5.) When obliged to pass or meet a lady who is riding without an escort, always do so at a moderate gait; this is an act of politeness and consideration which may prevent her steed from becoming fractious.

(6.) When passing by a horseman who is leading another[301] [302] horse, never ride by him on the side of the led animal, for if you do the latter will be apt to kick or plunge, and become unruly. This precaution is essential for the safety of the horsewoman, as well as for the better management of the led horse by the horseman. In a crowded place it will be better to wait until there is sufficient room to pass without hindrance.

(7.) Give assistance to a companion, or other lady rider, when it is indispensable for her safety, but do not give advice unless directly requested. And if, when you are riding a fractious horse, assistance be politely offered, do not decline it.

(8.) In city, town, or village, always ride at a moderate gait.

(9.) Be extremely careful never to ask for a friend's horse to ride, but always wait until the animal is freely offered, and when accepted, do not follow the advice contained in the horseman's proverb,—"With spurs of one's own and the horse of a friend, one can go where he pleases."

(10.) Before setting out for a ride, in company with other lady riders, the equestrienne, after having mounted, should move a short distance away from the others, and then keep her horse perfectly quiet and steady; by this course the neighboring horses will not be apt to become uneasy and restive while her companions are mounting.

(11.) Always, when with others, begin the ride at a moderate gait. A number of horses, fresh from the stable, when assembled together, are apt, if started on a gallop, to become too highly excited; and it will always be better to have them start slowly.

(12.) Should a lady be a better horsewoman than her companions, and be riding a horse superior to theirs, she should restrain him, and not allow him to be constantly in[303]advance of the others. It will be more courteous for her to follow the lead of her companions, and to consult with them as to the kind and rapidity of gait most agreeable to them. The preceding rules of politeness and propriety will be readily understood and appreciated. A lady under no circumstances will forget her tact and consideration for others.

(13.) In riding up hill the body should be inclined forward, and the bridle-hand be advanced, in order to give the horse space to extend his head and neck, as it is natural for him to do under such circumstances. In case the ascent be very steep, the rider may support herself by holding, with her right hand, to her horse's mane, but never to the off-pommel, because her weight may cause the saddle to slip backward.

(14.) In riding down hill the body must be inclined more or less backward, in proportion to the steepness of the hill, and as the horse lowers his head upon the commencement of the descent, the rider must advance her bridle-hand just enough barely to feel his mouth. Timid and awkward riders, on descending a hill, are apt to confine the horse's head too much, thus keeping it too high, and preventing him from freely stepping out, as well as from placing his feet firmly upon the ground. By doing this, they are likely to bring about the very catastrophe they are trying to avoid, namely, a stumble and a fall. Never ride at a rapid gait when going down hill.

(15.) It is always customary to keep to the left when passing by others on horseback or in vehicles, who are going in the same direction as the rider; and in passing those who are approaching, to keep to the right. But, in the latter instance, should anything be present that might cause the horse to shy, and a declivity, ditch, or other source of danger be on the right, while none exists on the left, it will then be safer for the rider to take the left side.

[304]

(16.) When crossing a stream, or when allowing one's horse to drink from it, a watchful eye should be kept upon him, especially in warm weather, lest he attempt to take an impromptu bath. If he begins to paw the water, or bend his knees, the rider must raise his head, give him a sharp stroke with the whip, and hurry him on.

(17.) After severe exercise, or when the horse is very warm, he should neither be fed nor be allowed to drink until a sufficient time has passed to enable him to become composed, rested, and cool. Many a valuable steed has been lost because his mistress did not know this simple, but highly important rule. Again, a horse should never be ridden at a fast gait just after he has eaten a meal, or taken a good drink; he should be allowed at least an hour in which to have his meal digested.

(18.) A horse should never be allowed to drink from a public trough, if it can possibly be avoided; and when he is permitted to do so, the trough should first be emptied and then filled anew. Horses often contract serious diseases from these public drinking-places.

(19.) When riding over a rough road, the horse's mouth should only be lightly felt, and he should be allowed to have his own way in selecting the safest places upon which to step.

(20.) When it is observed that the horse is moving uneasily, at the same time violently twitching his tail, or giving a kick outward or under him, the rider may be certain that something is hurting him, and should immediately dismount, loosen the saddle-girths, and carefully inspect the girths, the saddle, and parts touched by them to ascertain whether a nail be loosened from the saddle, the skin be pinched or abraded, the hair be pulled upon by the girths, or whether some hard object has become placed beneath the saddle, etc.; she should also carefully examine the head-stall and bit, to[305] see that all is right about the horse's head; after having removed or diminished the irritating cause, she should carefully readjust both saddle and girths.

(21.) If, when riding rapidly, it be observed that the horse is breathing with difficulty and with a strange noise, or that his head and ears are drooping, the rider should immediately stop him, as he has been driven too hard, and is on the point of falling.

(22.) A lady's horse should never be placed in harness, because in order to pull a load he will be obliged to throw his weight forward, thus spoiling the lightness of his saddle gaits.

(23.) When turning a corner the horse should not be drawn around by the reins; these should merely indicate the desired direction for the turn, and should never be drawn upon more than will bring that eye of the animal which is toward the direction of the turn into view of the rider.

(24.) Should a horse which is usually spirited move languidly, and, during warm, or moderately cold weather, have his hair stand out and appear rough, particularly about the head and neck, or should he frequently cough, it would be better to relinquish the ride, have him returned to the stable, and a warm bran-mash given to him as quickly as possible. It may be that he has contracted only a cold that can be checked by prompt measures. But should he continue to grow worse, a veterinary surgeon should be speedily summoned. Be very firm and decided in not permitting the groom to administer his favorite patent medicines, because such nostrums are as liable to occasion injury to animals as similar preparations are to human beings.

(25.) A few observations with regard to shoeing a horse may not be amiss. It may happen when riding on a country road, that one of the horse's shoes will come off, and the rider be obliged to resort to the nearest rural blacksmith to[306] have it replaced. In such case she will find that some knowledge on her part of the manner in which a shoe should be fitted to a horse's foot will prove very useful. The blacksmith should not be permitted to cut the frog (the soft and elastic substance in the middle of the foot) of the foot, but should leave it entirely alone, and pare around the margin of the hoof just enough to adjust the shoe evenly and firmly. Country blacksmiths, as well as many in cities, are very fond of paring and rasping the horse's hoof, as they think they can make a neater fit of the shoe by such a course. An eminent writer on the subject of shoeing states that, except in case of disease, undue paring and rasping are never indulged in by persons who understand how to fit a shoe to the horse's feet properly; he also observes: "This is paring and rasping the horse's foot till it be small enough to fit the shoe, rather than kindle a fire and forge a new set which shall just suit the feet of the animal. It may to some readers seem like a jest, to write seriously about the horse's shoes being too tight; but it is, indeed, no joke to the quadruped which has to move in such articles. The walk is strange, as though the poor creature were trying to progress, but could obtain no bearing for its tread. The legs are all abroad, and the hoofs no sooner touch the ground than they are snatched up again. The head is carried high, and the countenance denotes suffering. It is months before the horse is restored to its normal condition."

(26.) There is not the least necessity for stables being the foul smelling places they so frequently are, for if the hostler and his assistants perform their duties properly all offensive odors will be banished. A foul atmosphere in a stable, besides being repulsive to visitors, is, not unfrequently, the cause of blindness and other diseases of the horse, who will also carry the odor in his hair and communicate it to the clothing of his rider as well as to her saddle. For these reasons, a[307] lady should always positively insist that the stable as well as the horse should be kept perfectly clean and free from obnoxious exhalations. Attention to cleanliness, and a free use of disinfectants will bring about this highly desirable result.

(27.) After a ride, the saddle should always be aired, and placed where the sun's rays can fall upon its under surface. After exercise that causes the horse to perspire freely, the saddle should not be removed until he has become cool; this will prevent him from having a sore back, from which he often suffers when this precaution is neglected.

(28.) When a lady stops in her ride to visit a friend, she should always attend to her horse herself—be sure that he is properly hitched; that in warm weather he is fastened in a shady place, and that in cold weather he is protected, as far as possible, from the cold, as well as from wind, rain, or snow. It will sometimes happen, especially in the country, that, instead of being hitched, the horse will be allowed to remain free, but within some inclosure, that he may nibble the grass; in this instance, the saddle should always be removed, as otherwise he may roll upon it. A city horse, when ridden into the country, should not be allowed to eat grass, from a mistaken idea that it will be a good treat for him, for, as he is not accustomed to it, it will be very apt to injure him.

(29.) After a good seat and attitude in the saddle have been obtained, more freedom is allowable; should the rider have occasion to speak or to look aside, she should never move her shoulders, but only her head, and this momentarily, because it is required that a good lookout in front be kept up, to discover and avoid obstacles.

(30.) Delicate persons who desire to derive benefit from horseback riding in the country should select suitable hours in which to pursue this exercise. The intense heat of a summer noon should be avoided, as well as the evening dew,[308] the imperceptible dampness of which will penetrate the clothing and, perhaps, implant the germ of some serious malady. Riding upon a country road in the noon heat of a summer day, where there is little or no shade, will tan and roughen the finest complexion, will overheat the blood, and will occasion fatigue instead of pleasure. An hour or two after sunrise or before sunset will be found the more pleasant and healthful periods of the day for this exercise. Riding in the country, when enjoyed at proper hours, is a sure brightener of the complexion, aerates and purifies the blood, and imparts wonderful tone to the nervous and muscular systems. Yet, in their great fondness for this exercise, ladies frequently carry it to excess, making their rides far too long.

(31.) What to do with the whip, when making a call, has puzzled many a lady rider. Shall it be left outside, where it may be lost, or shall it be taken into the parlor, where its belligerent appearance will be entirely out of place? This much mooted question can soon be settled by the gentleman who assists the lady to dismount; he will usually understand what is required, and take charge of it himself. Or, in the absence of a cavalier, the whip may be handed to the groom who attends to the horse, or to the porter who waits upon the door. But should no groom or porter be present, it may be placed in some convenient and secure spot, as would be done with a valuable umbrella.

(32.) Before mounting her horse, a lady should always pat his head and speak kindly to him, and, after the ride, should express her satisfaction in the same manner. The horse will fully appreciate these manifestations. Many persons consider a horse a mere living, working machine, yet it has been satisfactorily ascertained, by those who have investigated the matter, that this machine has feeling, affection, and a remarkable memory; that it appreciates favors, has a high sense of gratitude, and never forgets an injury.

[309]

(33.) The secret of secure and graceful riding is a correctly balanced seat in the saddle, one perfectly independent of reins or stirrup, and without exaggerations of any kind, whether the carelessness or indifference of the instinctive rider, or the affected, pedantic stiffness of the antiquated *haut école.* While maintaining a free, easy, yet elegant attitude, the rider should present to the spectator such an appearance of security and perfect equilibrium that it will seem as if no conflicting movements of the horse could throw her from the saddle. Carelessness and indifference cause the rider to look indolent and slovenly, while an affected, exaggerated stiffness and preciseness give her a ridiculous appearance, and destroy the pleasing effect of an otherwise correct seat.

(34.) Go quickly in the walk, quickly and regularly in the trot, and gently in the gallop. And bear well in mind the following supplication of the horse:—

"In going up hill, trot me not;
In going down hill, gallop me not;
On level ground, spare me not;
In the stable, forget me not."

All women are capable of enjoying the healthful exercise of horseback riding excepting those who may be suffering from disease. Every lady who has the means, whether young or advanced in years, should learn riding, for its sociability, healthfulness, and pleasure, without regard to her bodily conformation. It is folly to deprive one's self of this high enjoyment and captivating exercise, simply because one is no longer young, has only an ordinary figure, or because some persons appear to better advantage in the saddle, and ride with more ease and grace. According to such reasoning, one might as well cease to exist. If a lady cannot attain perfection, she can strive to come as near to it as possible, and if she secures a correct seat in the saddle, and a[310] suitable horse, she will present a decidedly better appearance than one who, although having the slender, elegant figure so well adapted to the saddle, yet rides in a crooked, awkward attitude, or on a rough moving horse.

To become a complete horsewoman it is not necessary to begin the exercise in childhood. The first lessons may be taken in the twelfth year, though many of our best horsewomen did not begin to practice until they were eighteen years old, and some not until after they were married. Riding-teachers state that persons past their first youth who have never ridden learn much more readily, and become better riders than those who, though younger, have been riding without instruction, and in an incorrect manner, and, consequently, have contracted habits very difficult to eradicate.

Before closing this part of the work, there is one subject to which the author would earnestly invite attention. When a lady possesses a horse which has been long in her service, and been treated with the kindest and most loving care, and she finds that this faithful servant is becoming old and stiff, or that, from some accident, he has become almost useless to her, she should not part with him by selling him, for the ones to buy him will be those who have no sympathy for a horse and do not know how to treat him properly, but purchase him for hard and severe labor; their poverty compelling them to this course, as they cannot afford to buy any but old and maimed horses of very little value. To a well-treated and trained animal, the change from caresses to harsh treatment, from the pleasant task of carrying the light form of his mistress to the hardest of drudgery, must be acutely felt. The horse which has been kindly and intelligently managed is one of the most sensitive of living creatures, and has been known to refuse all feed and die from starvation, when placed under the charge of a cruel and ignorant master.

When the lady finds her favorite steed permanently useless,[311] and cannot afford him an asylum in which to pass the remainder of his days in rest and freedom from labor, she should have some merciful hand end the life that it would be cruel to prolong in the hands of a hard master, simply for the few dollars that might be obtained for him. To thus destroy the animal may appear heartless, but, in reality, is an act of mercy; as it is much better for him to die a quick, painless death, than to be sold to a life of toil, pain, and cruelty, in which, perhaps, he may pass mouths, if not years, of a living death.

In terminating the present volume, the writer ventures to express the hope that her appeal to American women to seek health, beauty, and enjoyment in the saddle will not be passed by with indifference, and that the lady rider, after a careful perusal and due consideration of the instructions herein laid down for her benefit, may be awakened to a spirit of enthusiasm, and an endeavor "to well do that which is worth doing at all." To gain a knowledge of horsewomanship is by no means a mysterious matter confined to only a favored few, but is, on the contrary, within the reach of all. The requirements necessary to manage the horse are soon learned, but, as is the case with every other accomplishment, it is practice that makes perfect. Practice alone, however, without study or instruction, will never produce a finished rider; and study without practice will rarely accomplish anything. But when study and practice are judiciously combined, they will enable one to reach the goal of success, which every earnest rider will strive to attain.

In the endeavor to render the instructions and explanations in this work as clear and comprehensible as possible, many repetitions have unavoidably occurred; but as the book was more especially designed to instruct beginners, as well as those self-taught riders who have not had the[312] advantage of a teacher, it was thought advisable not to leave any point in doubt, but as far as possible to render each subject independent of the others, and strongly to impress many essential points upon the mind of the reader.

To a majority of my countrywomen, with their natural tact and grace, it was only deemed necessary to point out their errors in riding; attention once called to them would, it was believed, undoubtedly lead to their prompt correction, and these riders would then cease to be victims of ignorance, constantly upon the verge of danger from incorrect methods of riding, and soon be able to excel in that most desirable and fascinating of all womanly accomplishments, secure and graceful horseback riding.

This has been the principal object of the author, who would not only have women ride well and elegantly, but with the confidence and enjoyment that true knowledge always imparts. Having spent so many happy hours in the saddle herself, she wishes others to experience a similar happiness, and if a perusal of these unpretending pages will create a zeal among her countrywomen for this delightful and invigorating exercise, and enable them to enjoy it in its highest sense, it will prove a source of much gratification to her, and she will rest satisfied that her efforts have not been in vain.

[313]

GLOSSARY
OF TERMS USED IN HORSEMANSHIP.

Aids: The various methods employed by a rider to command the horse, and urge him to move forward, backward, etc., and in such gaits as may be desired. The superior aids are the hands acting through the medium of the reins; the inferior aids are the leg and whip. See *Effects.*

Appui, Fr. *Support:* The "give and take" movements, by which the horse is supported in his gait, called "appui of the hand." The sensation of the pressure of the bit upon the bars of the horse's mouth, experienced by the rider's hand. *Appui of the Collar:*The slope or talus presented in front at the union of the crest of the neck with the shoulders.

Attacks: Methods for urging or inducing the horse to enter upon any gait or motion required. See *Aids.*

Bars: The upper part of the gums (in a horse) that bears no teeth, and which is located on each side of the lower jaw. This part lies between the grinders (back double teeth) and the tusks; or, in mares and in horses deprived of tusks, between the grinders and the incisors (front cutting teeth). It is against this part, the bars, that the curb-bit rests. See *Cheek of the Bit.*

Bear to the right: To keep the right leg, from hip to knee, as stationary as possible, by downward pressure upon the right side of the saddle seat, and between the first and second pommels, at the same time keeping a firm knee-grasp upon the second pommel without hanging upon it; by this means, the rider guards against inclining to the left, a movement very apt to be produced by her position in the saddle and the motion of her horse. The body of the rider must be maintained in an erect position all the time she is bearing to the right. See *Incline to the Right.*

Boot: A term sometimes applied to that part of the saddle-girths or[314] flaps back of the rider's leg, and at which the horse may attempt to kick; also applied to the inferior portion of the rider's leg.

Bridle-hand: The left hand. When both hands hold the reins they are called the *bridle-hands.*

Bridoon: The snaffle-bit and rein, when used in connection with the curb-bit, but acting independently of it. The two bits together in the horse's mouth are called "the bit and bridoon," or "the curb and bridoon."

Bringing up to the bridle, also *Kept well up to the bridle:* To place the horse's head up and in position, so that when proper tension or pressure is made upon his mouth he will readily obey the reins. Some horses require stronger pressure than others, as stated under *Correspondence.*

Cannon bone, also *Shank:* The long bone situated between the knee and the fetlock joint on the front part of each fore-leg of the horse.

Canon: That part of a bit, on each side, that rests upon the bars of a horse's mouth when the bit is correctly placed.

Cantle: The somewhat elevated ridge at the back part of the saddle-seat.

Cheek of the Bit, also *Bars of the Bit:* The external straight or curved rods (levers) forming the sides of a curb-bit, and which, when the bit is in the horse's mouth, are applied along the outer sides of his mouth, the reins being attached to their lower extremities. That part of these rods situated below the bit in the month is called "the lower bar," or "cheek," and that portion above the bit, "the upper bar," or "cheek."

Chin-groove: The transverse furrow in which the curb-chain rests, on the under surface of a horse's lower jaw, at the back part of the lower lip. Also called "curb-groove."

Collected canter: A canter in good form.

Correspondence: The degree of rein-tension made by the hand of the rider upon her horse's mouth, which, when properly established, creates a correspondence between her hand and the animal's mouth, so that the slightest movement of the one is immediately felt by the other; in all cases this correspondence must first be had before any utility can be obtained from the "give and take" movements. Some horses require a greater degree of tension for this purpose than others, according to their training and the range of sensibility of their mouths.

Croup: The hind-quarters of the horse, from and including the loins to the commencement of the tail. This term is also applied by some[315] to the upper part of the animal's back, where the haunches and body come in contact.

Curb-bit, also *Lever-bit:* A bit with a straight or curved lever or rod attached on each side, designed for the purpose of restraining the horse.

Curb-chain: A chain attached to the upper bar or cheek of the curb-bit, and passed along the chin-groove, from one side of the bit to the other.

Curb-hook: A hook attached to the curb-chain, and designed to fasten it to the upper bar of the curb-bit; there are two of these hooks, one on each side of the bit.

Decompounded: Taken to pieces; each act, movement, or part of a whole or group, by or of itself.

Defend: A horse is said to defend himself when he refuses to obey, or attempts to bite, kick, etc.; he resists, contends.

Defenses: The resistances made by a horse when required to do anything, or when he is ignorant of the acts or movements demanded of him; he becomes alarmed, injured, or malicious, and employs his defenses.

Double bridle: The reins of the curb-bit and bridoon, when both bits are placed together in the horse's mouth.

Dumb-jockey: A couple of stout sticks or poles, crossed in the form of the letter x, and fastened upon the saddle; the reins are attached to the upper ends of these, and a hat may be placed upon one of them. Used in training colts.

Effects: Movements made by the hands, often aided by the leg or whip, which serve to urge the horse forward, backward, to the right, or left; indications.

Equestrian: A gentleman rider on horseback.

Equestrienne: A lady rider on horseback.

Equine: From *equus*, Lat. A horse; pertaining to a horse.

Equitation: Horseback riding.

False pannels: Pannels are stuffed pads or flaps, attached to and beneath certain parts of the saddle, in order to prevent these from injuring the horse; when these stuffed pads can be fastened to, or removed from the saddle at pleasure, they are termed "false pannels."

Fetlock: The tuft of hair that grows upon the back part of the fetlock joints of many horses' legs, and which hides the ergot or stub of soft horn that lies behind and below the pastern joint.

Fetlock joint: The joint between the cannon and the upper pastern bone of each foot.

[316]

Force the hands: The hands are said to be forced when the horse throws his head downward, pulling upon the reins so as to cause the rider to support the weight of the animal's head; sometimes this is effected so suddenly as to jerk the reins out of her hands.

Forehand: All that part of the horse in front of the rider.

Get out of condition: A horse is said to be in "good condition" when he is well, fresh, and sound; the reverse of this is termed "out of condition."

Girths: Stout straps or bands passed from one side of the saddle and underneath the horse's abdomen to the other side, where they are buckled tight and fast; they are designed to keep the saddle securely upon the horse's back.

Give and take: The traction and relaxation of the reins made by the fingers, and which must correspond with the movements of the horse's head; this action keeps up a correspondence with the horse's mouth, and at the same time supports him in his gait.

Hand: The height of a horse is usually measured by hands, four inches being equal to one hand. A rider is said to "have hands" when she knows how to use her hands correctly in controlling the horse by means of the reins.

Haunches: When a horse is made to throw his weight chiefly upon his hind-quarters, he is said to be "well placed on his haunches," and will then move more lightly upon his fore-legs. The haunch-bones are three in number, the superior one of which is firmly united to the spinal column (backbone) near its posterior extremity; the lower one on each side forms a joint with the thigh bone, passing downward in a more or less oblique direction. The obliquity of these bones enables the horse to place the muscles of the part in a position to act with greater advantage and power, and the degree of this obliquity serves to distinguish the thorough from the low bred, it being greater in the former. Wide haunches and broad loins are indications of strength and speed.

Hippic: Of, belonging to, or relating to the horse.

Hock, also *Tarsus:* The part or joint between the cannon or shank bone and the lower thigh or gaskin of the hind-leg: it consists of six bones; the part at this joint that projects backward and somewhat inward is called the "point of the hock." The hock is an important part of a horse, as any unhealthy or diseased condition of it will prevent him from resting on his haunches, and will thereby interfere with his free action in the canter and gallop.

[317]

Immobility: A disease in which the horse becomes unable to move, probably referable to the nervous system.

Incline to the right, or *to the left:* This differs from "bearing to the right," which see. It means, to incline the body, from the hips upward, to the right (or to the left), either when turning or riding in a circle.

In confidence: A horse is confident, or in confidence, when he completely surrenders his own will, and implicitly trusts to his rider without dreaming of resistance.

Inward rein: In turning or circling, the "inward rein," as well as the "inward leg," is the one on the same side as that toward which the horse turns, or the one toward the centre of the circle of which the turn forms an arc.

Legs well bent: See "*Well-bent hind-legs*."

Lip-strap, or *Curb-strap:* Two small straps stitched to the curb-bit, designed to prevent a horse from taking the cheek of this bit into his mouth; an unnecessary appendage when the cheek is curved.

Lunge-line: A long strap or cord attached to the nose-band of the cavesson or head-stall of a horse in training, by means of which the trainer exercises and instructs him while he is moving around in circles.

Near-side: The left side. *Near-pommel:* The second pommel, on the left side of the side-saddle; the second pommel of the old-fashioned saddle was called the "near-pommel," and the name still attaches to it. The "third pommel" is variously called the "leaping head" and the "hunting-horn," and is located on the left side of the saddle and below the second pommel.

Off-side: The right side. *Off-pommel:* The pommel on the right side of the saddle.

Outward rein: In turning or circling, the "outward rein," as well as the "outward leg," is the one opposite to the direction toward which the horse turns.

Overreaching, also *Forging, Clinking:* Is when a horse in moving forward strikes the heel or back part of a fore-foot with the toe or front part of the shoe of the hind-foot. When the stride of the hind-legs is carried so far forward as to strike the coronet or upper part of the hoof, it is then termed a "tread."

Pirouette: A movement in which a horse turns around without changing his place, the hind-leg of the side toward which he moves forming the pivot upon which he supports himself.

[318]

Port of the bit: The arched part in the centre of the curb-bit.

Resistances: See *Defenses.*

Retroacting: A horse retroacts when, in his volts, he steps aside, bearing his croup to the centre,—also when he backs toward an obstacle and fixedly remains there, against the will of his rider; and also when he suddenly throws himself upon his hocks at the moment his rider checks or stops him.

Ring-bar of the saddle: A bar attached beneath the saddle-flap on the left side and at its upper part, over which the stirrup-leather rolls.

Saddle-tree: The skeleton or solid frame of a saddle, upon which the pommels, leather, padding, etc., are properly disposed.

Snaffle-bit: Is the mildest bit used in driving a horse: there are two kinds, the plain snaffle and the twisted, and the latter form may be made to act very severely.

Surcingle: A wide band of cloth or leather, of sufficient length to pass around the body of a horse, and employed either to keep a blanket upon him, or to keep down the flaps of the saddle or the shabrack.

Thrown forward upon his shoulders: A horse is said to be thrown in this manner when, in moving, he throws his weight chiefly upon his shoulders and fore-legs instead of upon his hind-quarters; he is then also said to "go heavy on his fore-legs."

Turn upon the shoulders: A horse is said to "turn upon his shoulders" when he throws his weight upon his fore-legs during the act of turning; it is a disunited movement.

Tusks, also *Tushes:* These are the canine teeth, two in each jaw, which grow between the grinders (back double teeth) and the incisors (front cutting teeth), being closer to the latter than to the former. They are frequently missing. Their uses are not well known.

Volt: The movement of a horse while going sidewise in a circle, his croup being toward the centre. There are several varieties of volt. An *inverted* or *reversed volt* is when the head of the horse is kept toward the centre of the circle.

Well-bent hind-legs: A horse with straight hind-legs does not possess good and easy movements; but if these limbs be well bent, he can be well placed on his haunches, and be easily collected, so that his action will be true and pleasant. See *Haunches.*

Yield the hands: Is to give the horse more rein by advancing the hands without allowing the reins to slip. To *give a free rein* is to allow the animal all the length of rein he requires without any traction or opposition.

[319]

INDEX.

FOOTNOTES:

[1]A very interesting work, by C. A. Piétrement, has recently been issued in France, entitled *Les chevaux dans les temps prehistorique et historique.* The author shows that wild horses were hunted and eaten by man in the rough stone age. He also determines in what European and Asiatic regions the eight extant horse families were domesticated, and traces their various wanderings over the earth, deducing many interesting facts from the history of their migrations.

[2]"The Bedouin (and every other race of Orientals that I am acquainted with seems to possess somewhat the same quality) exhibits a patience towards his horse as remarkable as is the impatience and roughness of the Englishman.... In his (the Oriental's) mental organization some screw is tight which in the English mind is loose; he is sane on a point where the Englishman is slightly cracked, and he rides on serene and contented where the latter would go into a paroxysm of swearing and spurring. I have seen an Arab horse, broken loose at a moment when our camp was thronged with horses brought for sale, turn the whole concern topsy-turvy, and reduce it to one tumult of pawing and snorting and belligerent screeching; and I never yet saw the captor when he finally got hold of the halter show the least trace of anger, or do otherwise than lead the animal back to his picket with perfect calmness. Contrast this with the 'job' in the mouth and the kick in the ribs and the curse that the English groom would bestow under similar circumstances, and you have, in a great measure, the secret of the good temper of the Arab horse in Arab hands."—*Blackwood's Magazine*, 1859.

[3]"There is, however, a medium in this, and the advantage of length in the arm will depend on the use to which the horse is applied. The lady's horse, the cavalry horse, every horse in which prancing action is esteemed a beauty, and in which utility is, to a certain degree, sacrificed to appearance, must not be too long in the arm. If he is long there, he will be proportionally short in the leg; and although this is an undoubted excellence, whether speed or continuance is regarded, the short leg will not give the grand and imposing action which fashion may require. In addition to this, a horse with short legs may not have quite so easy an action as another whose length is in the shank rather than in the arms."—*W. Youatt.*

[4]It is stated in this paragraph that the *marks on the reins* should be "nearly even," or "nearly on a line with each other," because, in its passage under the little finger, across the hand, and on the outside of the right rein, the left one will be shortened so that its marking will be about half an inch nearer the bit than that of the right one; consequently, in order to make the pressure upon the horse's mouth even, the right rein will have to be shortened to the extent named.

[5]The bridle-hand being in the *original position* for the double bridle, the curb should be brought into action by a turn of the wrist, which will carry the little finger in toward the waist; and this, in conjunction with the leg and whip, will collect the horse.

[6]If the horse be tender in the mouth the snaffle-reins had better be used in backing; if not, the curb.

[7]By "bearing to the right" is not meant an inclination of the body to this side, but a resistance sufficient to keep the body from inclining toward the left. As hereafter stated, trotting in a circle to the *right* will be found an excellent exercise to teach one this bearing.

[8]If the leap be a very high one, the left foot may be thrust a little more forward to enable the rider to lean back as far as is necessary.